BULLY'S
DARKNESS

NICOLA JANE

Editor: Rebecca Vazquez, Dark Syde Books

Formatting: Nicola Miller

Cover Design: Crimson Cruz

Spelling Note

Please note, this author resides in the United Kingdom and is using British English. Therefore, some words may be viewed as incorrect or spelled incorrectly, however, they are not.

TRIGGER WARNING - PLEASE READ

This book is part of the Royal Bastards MC, if you are easily offended, this isn't the place for you. If you decide to jump in anyway, and then get offended, put it in writing to the club's president, Bully, and he'll ignore you, mainly because he doesn't give a crap.

Acknowledgements

Thank you to all my wonderful readers. Without you, I wouldn't be doing what I love x

Also, a huge thank you to the Royal Bastards for letting me be part of their world. It's a huge honour and I hope I've done the story justice.

Social Media

I love to hear from my readers and if you'd like to get in touch, you can find me here . . .

<u>My Facebook Page</u>

<u>My Facebook Readers Group</u>

<u>Bookbub</u>

<u>Instagram</u>

<u>Goodreads</u>

<u>Amazon</u>

CONTENTS

Playlist

no tears left to cry - Ariana Grande

traitor – Olivia Rodrigo

Delicate – Taylor Swift

Please Please Please – Sabrina Carpenter

That's So True – Gracie Abrams

Illegal – PinkPantheress

Family Matters – Skye Newman

Sapphire – Ed Sheeran

back to friends - sombr

Mr. Brightside – The Killers

Iris – Goo Goo Dolls

Numb – Linkin Park

Can't Stop – Red Hot Chili Peppers

Love The Hell Out Of You – Lewis Capaldi

CHAPTER ONE

Olivia

"It doesn't take a genius to know why you're grinning like a Cheshire cat this morning." Bria throws her arm around my shoulder and kisses me on the cheek. "What time is he getting out?"

I peer into my handbag for the third time to check I have my phone and car keys. "They won't give me a time," I reply, zipping it closed, "so I'm just going to head over and wait."

She frowns. "Well, that's ridiculous," she says, running her fingers through her dark brown hair and scraping it back into a ponytail. "Why can't they just give you a time?"

I shrug. "You know what the prison is like, they don't make anything easy." I grab my bag and jacket.

"Do you want me to come with you?"

I shake my head. I've been waiting for five years for this moment. Five long years. I've had time to plan every last detail, even down to the hotel where I'm going to surprise Bully with an entire night of . . . well, *me*. I smile at the thought.

"Livvy," she says, and I look over to where she's filling her cup with hot water. "I know you're excited but be careful. I love you."

"Relax," I say, adding a reassuring smile. "Things will be good this time around. He's promised."

I check my watch and then my mobile phone. It's almost five o'clock, and I've been sitting here waiting since ten this morning. The gate has opened a few times to release prisoners into the loving arms of their relatives, but not one of them has been Bully.

As it slides back for the fifth time, I grab my bag and get out of the car. This has to be him.

I straighten my dress as I make my way over then run my fingers through my hair to loosen the curls I'd spent an hour doing at six a.m. when I was too excited to sleep.

The prison guard pops his head out, glancing over me before stepping back. I hold my breath in anticipation, smiling wide. It fades the second a tall man steps out. A whistle from somewhere behind me gets his attention, and he gives a relieved sigh as he heads off in that direction. The guard begins to close the gates.

"Excuse me," He pauses, "I'm waiting for my fiancé."

"That was the last of them today, love," he tells me, once again moving the gates closed.

"But it's definitely today," I push, stepping closer.

He sighs heavily. "Name?"

"Liam Bull."

He glances down at a clipboard. "He was released first thing," he tells me. "Nine-thirty."

I frown, my mind racing with questions. If he'd headed home, Bria would have called me. Unless . . . I feel tension building in my chest. "Do you know if he was picked up?"

He glances behind him, looking mildly irritated. "Charlie, did you see if Bully got picked up this morning?" He waits for the reply that I can't make out before looking back to me and nodding. "Yep, he got picked up. Bikers, apparently."

I nod, my hands curling into tight balls of tension. "'Course he did," I mutter, rolling my eyes. *What did I expect?*

By the time I get home, I'm raging. Bully promised me he was done with that place. The Royal Bastards were the entire reason he was in prison.

Bria looks up when I enter the kitchen, frowning when she sees I'm alone. "How did it go?" she asks, concern lacing her features.

"Take a guess," I mutter, throwing my keys on the side and dropping down into a chair.

She sits up straighter. "He didn't get out?" She growls in frustration. "Fuck, Livvy, I knew he'd do this to you. This is exactly what happened the last time—"

I hold a hand up and shake my head. "He hasn't got extra time," I confirm. A year ago, he was given a twenty-four-month sentence added on to his current eight years for fighting. Luckily, with an appeal and some good behaviour, he's only served half his entire sentence. "He was let out this morning. The club picked him up."

"So, where have you been all day, with him at the club?"

I shake my head, foolishness creeping in as I take a breath. "I waited all day, and when he didn't show, I asked the guard, who told me he left at nine-thirty with bikers."

"Motherfuckers," she cries, pushing to her feet. "After everything he promised." She grabs my car keys. "You're not sitting around here waiting for him to call, Livvy. We're going to the clubhouse."

Bully

I take a calming breath, releasing it slowly as I run my eyes over my pride and joy—my Harley-Davidson Fatboy. Five years I've waited for this moment, and the second I throw my leg over and settle onto the leather seat, I groan in pleasure. I grip the handlebars and take another deep breath as the engine rumbles to life and the vibrations run through my body. Taz slaps me on the back, smirking. "Bet you missed her."

"Thanks for looking after her."

"Brother, you know I've got your back. I even had the prospects polish her up for you."

"I'm gonna ride out and see Liv," I tell him, and he winces. "What?"

"You got shit to deal with here first," he tells me, and I turn the bike off, my heart sinking with the sound of the engine. "Sorry, I know you want to go see your old lady, but Jameson is gonna call soon and he'll want to speak to you." I nod cos he's right. Jameson is the National Chapter President, and if he calls, you answer, no questions. "Have you thought about it?" he asks, and I shake my head.

My uncle Tony was the President up until two weeks ago, when he passed. Fucker came off his bike right into the path of a lorry. He never stood a chance. And seeing as I was his Vice President, with Taz only standing in while I was inside, Jameson wants me to step up and become the Nottingham Chapter's President.

"Of course, I want to," I admit. "It's been my dream since I was a kid watching Tony and my dad running this place. But Liv wants a different life now." My heart aches at the thought of the promises I'm already breaking by just being here. But when the club turned up first thing and she wasn't around, I assumed she'd sent them. It wasn't until I was back at the clubhouse that I realised she had no idea.

"Brother, she's made it clear the club is not part of her life anymore. The day you went down, she left and never looked back. Your uncle sent her money every week, and she returned it."

"I know all this," I mutter. Tony regularly updated me with his efforts to watch over my stubborn old lady. "She just needs time."

Sparrow, the club's prospect, sticks his head into the garage. "Bully, Jameson's on the phone in the pres's office."

I nod, getting off the bike to head inside. It feels weird being here without my uncle. He was like part of the furniture, starting this club up alongside my dad after they left the Army. When Dad died ten years ago, I wasn't ready to run things, so Tony stepped up, and he made a good president. The place won't be the same without him.

I stand at the desk, staring at the president's chair as I press the phone to my ear. "Pres, good to hear from you," I say.

"Son, it's good to hear your voice. I was damn sorry to hear about your uncle."

"Me too. I got to go to the funeral, even if it was in cuffs."

"We celebrated his life over here too," he tells me. "He was a good man, just like your father."

"I appreciate that, Pres."

"Let's cut the crap. You know why I'm calling." I smile, nodding, even though he can't see me. "I don't just let anyone take that title," he adds, "and you've got some big boots to fill. Are you ready for the challenge?"

I take a deep breath. "Yes, sir," I tell him. "I am."

"That's good news, Bully. I'll spread the word. Get settled and call me in a few days so we can pick up where your uncle left off."

I disconnect the call and place the phone back on the desk. Then I move the chair to one side. It doesn't feel right sitting in it just yet, and I vow to get another just as soon as I've spoken to the guys.

Church is an important affair. We discuss everything within these four walls and make some of the biggest decisions. Life and death have been discussed right here.

I run my fingers over the chips in the wood where the gavel has battered it and smile. As a kid, I watched my old man sitting right here making important decisions, and as I got older, I wondered how he made it look so easy. Then, when my uncle Tony—or Hawk, as the club knew him—took it on, he slipped right into the same role like it was nothing. So, why am I standing here feeling like the weight of the world is on my shoulders?

The door opens, and the men begin to filter in, each shaking my hand again, even though we did all this earlier when I got back. I wait patiently while they take their seats, still standing behind mine. *Mine.* It feels weird. When all eyes are on me, I square my shoulders and brace my hands on the table. "I just spoke to Jameson," I tell them. "I accepted his offer."

Taz stands, grinning wide and shaking my hand while slapping my shoulder. "That's good news, Pres," he says, and I almost shudder at the title. It's gonna take some time to get used to it. He turns to the rest. "We need to welcome our President in style," he says, and they cheer. "Someone get the bar open, it's gonna be a long night."

"I can take a wild guess who the VP is gonna be," says Smiler, his tone teasing.

I grin. "Who else would I have beside me?" I ask, slapping Taz on his back. He's been by my side since we were six years old. His dad, Rubble, was one of my dad's closest friends, and though he doesn't ride anymore, he still sits proudly at this table today.

Stilletto prances around in underwear, and I try to keep my eyes focused on Boss. He's a damn fine Road Captain, but fuck, he talks for England and is making it damn near impossible to not get distracted by the half-naked club whore.

Poison pours me a fourth glass of whiskey, and I'm seeing double. I haven't eaten since last night, and I haven't drunk for years, not unless you count the moonshine they made in that hell hole that tasted like piss water.

"Now you're the President, you get pick of the girls," she tells me, arching a brow. "Not that you didn't already."

I scoff. "My old lady might have something to say about that."

She smirks. "We both know the girls are discreet." She places the bottle of whiskey down and whistles, gaining the club whores' attention. "Gather here," she orders, and they assemble quickly, like they've practised this a million times. The women stand side by side, their bodies on show, covered by either skimpy outfits or sexy underwear. "I'm sure you remember Stiletto," says Poison, and Stiletto steps forward, biting on her bright red lower lip as she runs her eyes over me with a playful smirk.

"Next up is Poodle. She's new here." The blonde smiles seductively, popping a button on her already too tight top so it springs open to reveal her pushed-up cleavage.

"Karma's been here about a year," says Poison as the next woman steps forward. "She's popular amongst the guys, but her priority will always be you, of course." The last woman steps forward, and I run my eyes over her red lace underwear. Her nipples are visible, and my cock twitches to life. It's been too long, and having these women around, knowing I just have to say the word, is tempting.

"Well, look what the cat dragged in," yells a female voice I know so well, it's engrained in my brain even if I haven't heard it for five years.

I glance to my left and see Bria marching towards me. *Fuck.* "Bitches, you better make yourselves disappear before I unleash my claws," she adds, and Poison gives a nod. They rush off, and that's when I see her. Olivia. *My Liv.*

I stand, ignoring Bria and moving towards my old lady. Our eyes are locked, and the rest of the room fades away until it's just me and her, the way it was always supposed to be. And suddenly, I can breathe easy again.

CHAPTER TWO

Olivia

I don't want to nag. I've never been a nagger. My mum was terrible for it, always on my dad until he couldn't take any more and left us, never to be seen again. I think that's why I refuse to be like her. The fear of losing someone I love keeps me quiet. But as my eyes fix on Bully, I have an overwhelming need to punch him right in the face.

His smile is wide, his dimples showing. He knows what he's doing, trying to soften me with those blue eyes and his cheeky boy grin. But I refuse to let him worm his way out of this. "I waited," I say, stopping just out of his reach. "All day." I cross my arms over my chest, and he stuffs his in his pockets, probably to stop himself from grabbing me. "I watched men leaving, embracing their loved ones." Fuck knows if he touches me, I'll give in, and Bria would blow a gasket. "You didn't even call me."

I swore all the way over here that I would give him shit. She's right, I have to set expectations now. I feel Bria's appraising eyes on me, her smile smug as Bully's eyes beg me to forgive him.

I glance around, noting some of the other brothers watching our exchange with amusement. Because that's all I am to this club, a joke. "And I come here to find you, what . . ." I look to where Poison stands behind the bar, pretending to be busy when she's really listening in, "choosing a whore?" The words hurt my heart, and my voice cracks slightly with emotion.

"Shit, no, Liv, of course, I wasn't," he rushes to say, his hands breaking free from the constraints of his pockets.

I step back again, shaking my head. "You promised me things would change."

"Let's go into my office and I can explain."

I narrow my eyes. "*Your* office?" I repeat.

He winces. "A lot has happened since Tony passed."

I press my lips into a fine line. "Tell me you're not taking over."

Taz steps up behind Bully, slapping him on the back. "Come on, Liv, it's a time to celebrate. No hard feelings. Let's move forward."

I scoff, unable to stop the tears from filling my eyes. "Thanks, but I'll pass." I turn towards the exit, keeping my head down to avoid everyone's prying eyes. Bria rushes after me, falling into step beside me, and as we break out into the cool evening air, a sob escapes me. "Don't cry, Livvy," she whispers. "Don't let him see you cry."

I give a stiff nod, picking up my pace. "Give me the keys," I mutter, holding out my hand.

"Are you okay to drive?"

"Just give me the keys," I snap, and she pulls them from her pocket and holds them to me. A hand comes between us, snatching them, and I spin on my heel to face Bully.

"You're not leaving until we've talked," he says firmly.

"The fuck we're not," yells Bria, grabbing my hand and tugging me towards the gate. "We'll call a taxi."

"Liv," he growls, and I shudder at the tone of his voice.

"Ignore him," hisses Bria.

"Liv," he bellows, more sharply this time. "Don't you dare walk away from me."

I slow to a stop, keeping my head bowed. Tears drip uncontrollably, and Bria sighs heavily. "Every fucking time," she mutters, rolling her eyes. "Fine, go and talk, but I'm not going anywhere without you." And she sits on the wall by the gate.

I turn back to Bully. "Make it quick," I mutter.

"Come inside."

"No, Liam," I snap, finally looking at him. "Say what you have to say so I can end this and walk away."

He frowns, closing the gap between us. "You don't mean that."

"Say the words," I cry. "Tell me how you have no choice, Bully. Tell me how much this club means to you, how you love it more than you've ever loved me." I swipe my tears angrily. "Tell me how you're going to break every single promise you made to me."

"Why do I have to choose?" he yells, throwing his arms in the air. "Why can't I have both?"

"It's sad that the best years of our life together were the ones where you were in prison," I whisper.

"Because you were in control," he snaps, pointing his finger in my face. "You knew exactly where I was all the time, so you were happy."

"I knew you were safe," I cry. "I knew you weren't getting into trouble, or worse, sleeping with some slag."

His expression softens. "Those days are behind me."

"You said that about the club."

"Liv, my Uncle Tony died. What am I supposed to do?"

"Walk away," I scream. "Choose me."

Bully

I hate seeing her so sad and desperate. And thanks to me, I've seen it far too many times. "It runs in my veins," I mutter, shrugging.

"Where were they?" she demands, placing her hands on her hips. "When shit went down, where the fuck were they?"

"They were there for me, Liv," I argue. I feel Taz's presence to my right, filling his role without me even having to ask. "I know you think they pushed me to do what I did, but it was all on me."

She rolls her eyes. "You can't even see it."

"See what, Olivia?" Taz snaps. "Fuck, we've spent years listening to you bitching and whining about how life's so unfair. Truth is, we would all take a hit for the club cos that's our life. The fact you don't get that tells him all he needs to know."

She scoffs, fixing her eyes back on me, waiting for my response. "Jameson asked me himself," I say. "Do you know how important that is?" Liv gives a stiff nod then turns her back, heading towards where her sister is patiently waiting. "So, that's it?" I call after her.

"You made it perfectly clear where you stand the second you ditched me to get a ride home with them," she retorts.

Bria approaches, holding out her hand. "Keys," she orders.

I reluctantly hand them over. "Don't let her drive," I mutter. "She's too upset."

"I know how to take care of my sister," she hisses. "I've been doing it for five years."

"If you love her at all, you wouldn't let her walk away. You know this is where she belongs."

She grins. "And if you love her, you'd walk away from this place and put her first . . . for once." She stomps away, neither of them looking back.

Taz rests a hand on my shoulder. "It's shit, brother, but right now, we've got stuff to deal with that's way bigger than you getting your heart trampled on."

I roll my eyes, heading inside. "She's my old lady, Taz. Have some fucking respect."

I feel his grin in his words. "That President patch is already sounding good on you."

I stop by the bar. "Poison, send Birdy to my room in ten minutes." She gives a salute, her smile wide as I storm off to the office with Taz on my heels.

"You sure you wanna be doing that, Pres?" he asks as I drag a stool to the desk, leaving my uncle's chair to the side.

"I've not had my cock wet in years, brother, what do you think?"

He smirks, shrugging. "Your call."

"Right, fill me in." I've had regular calls with my uncle, and the brothers have all been visiting weekly, but now I'm in charge, I need to hear the bits they've kept from me. The bits they knew would send me over the edge and have me adding more time onto my sentence.

"It's not good, Pres," he admits, taking a seat opposite me. "The Bloody Scorpions have rooted here way quicker than we expected."

I frown. "What do you mean? It was only last week you said they'd been spotted."

His expression turns to guilt. "Hawk didn't want to add to your stress, and then he died and—"

"Just get to the point," I snap impatiently.

"They've been around for about two months. Their VP, Bullet, was with some of their guys in Spencer's bar. That place is full of dealers and trouble. The Pres ran it by Jameson, who said to run them out at the first opportunity. But then he got sick and . . . well, you know the rest."

"He's been dead two weeks," I hiss. "In the ground for seven days. What the fuck are the Scorpions still doing here?"

"It's been hard," he mutters.

"You sound like a bitch."

His eyes widen, and he eventually smirks. "I ain't no president. I didn't want to call the shots on this, Bull. Not without you."

I scrub my hand over my face, suddenly feeling tired. "I want everyone in church at eight a.m. Anyone who's late will spend a week on polishing duty." He arches a brow but chooses to stay quiet. Things are changing around here, starting with stricter rules.

I take the stairs two at a time and come to an abrupt stop outside my bedroom door. Five years seems so long since I've slept in a proper bed with a thick quilt and fluffy pillows, and as I push the door open, disappointment fills me to find Birdy sitting on the edge in nothing but her underwear and heels. I'd forgotten about my request for company.

She stands, smiling seductively. "You look stressed," she notes, stopping in front of me and placing her hand on my chest. "Let me help you with that." She slips her hand into mine, lacing our fingers, and I shudder. She's stunning, but she isn't Liv. Her hand slides over my lazy cock, who's clearly only in the mood for one woman.

"Forget it," I mutter, pushing her hand away. "I'm tired."

Her smile falters. "We can just lie down together and see where the night takes us," she suggests, but I'm already guiding her out the door.

"Another time."

I slam it and lean against it, growling in frustration. I could have any woman sucking my cock, but I only want one. "Damn it," I mutter, grabbing my jacket. "Stubborn fucking—" I head out, rushing through the main room to avoid questions.

CHAPTER THREE

Olivia

I down the third cocktail and wince at the burning aftertaste. I look around the table at my closest friends and smile. I'm lucky. All it took was a text message to have them all come together for a night out. A night where any mention of Bully or his stupid club is banned.

Bria leans closer. "Did I just see a smile?"

I laugh. "I was just thinking how lucky I am."

"That's the spirit. You're loved, Livvy, you don't need—"

"Don't say it," I cry, and she giggles, slapping her hand over her mouth. Everyone who's said it so far has had to down a shot of sours, and Bria is on her fifth.

Stacy grabs the bottle of sours and tops a shot glass anyway, ignoring Bria's protests. "You thought it, so it counts," she says, laughing. "Now, drink the damn shot."

I watch in amusement. "Thanks, ladies. I don't know what I'd do without you all," I say.

Laura grabs my hand and gives it a quick squeeze. "It's gonna be okay, Livvy."

I nod. "I can't believe I wasted five years of my life on him."

"Eight, if you count the three before he went inside," Bria says while Stacy tops up two shot glasses. I take mine and drink it, holding it out for a second refill because I'm about to break the rule again.

"I knew he wouldn't walk away completely," I explain, "but I thought he'd at least consider me in his plans. I waited all day to see him. I even booked us a—"

"Night at the Marriott," the girls sing-song, and I laugh.

"Sorry, I'm just so pissed about the entire thing. I thought we were gonna have a great night planning our future."

"You should shag someone else," Bria announces, looking around the bar.

I screw my nose up. "It's not even been a few hours."

"She's right, Bria," Lisa cuts in. "Tonight is about forgetting men."

"We're single, we should have some fun," Bria argues as she slides from the booth. "I'm going to check out the talent in this place."

"Don't come back until you find us a wealthy group of hot men," Claudia shouts after her.

I roll my eyes, shaking my head as I push to stand. "I'm going to find a bathroom. Please don't let my sister embarrass herself."

As I'm waiting in line, my handbag vibrates, and I reach in for my mobile. The number is unknown, so I cancel it. Seconds later, a text message comes through, and I groan.

> **Unknown: Save my new number. Where are you?**

I save it. *Of course, I do.*

> **Me: I'm not telling you and I don't need your number.**

> **Bully: I'm coming to find you. I need to see you.**

> **Me: We're over. Leave me the fuck alone.**

I stuff my phone away, anger coursing through me that he'd think it was that simple to sort our shit out. He's proved he can't change. The only thing I'm surprised about is that he's not holed up in his room with a club whore.

When I get back to the table, Bria is back with a group of men, and I groan dramatically. "Here she is," cries Bria, smiling wide as she waves her hand in my direction. The men make a clearing, and I take my seat at the table, avoiding eye contact. "This is my younger sister, Livvy."

"Olivia," I correct, risking a glance up. They're not the usual type of men you find on a night out in Nottingham. Especially in a dive bar like Tudor's.

The one nearest to me holds out his hand, and I take it without question. A smile pulls at his lips. "Darren," he greets. "Your sister said you need cheering up."

I shake my head, feeling my cheeks redden slightly. "She's drunk. Ignore her."

He slides in beside me, forcing me to move along the booth. "She was pretty insistent."

I watch as Bria chats with one of his friends. He's definitely her type, with tattoos, piercing green eyes, and broad shoulders, but looking at the group, they're all similar in description. "Are you brothers?" I ask, and he smirks.

"Of sorts."

Dread fills me. "Bikers," I confirm, my heart rate picking up.

"And what do you know about bikers?" he asks, a smile still playing on his lips.

"Way more than I want to," I say firmly. "Bria," she looks over, "we need to go." The rest of the women are also chatting with the men, and I sigh in frustration. I'm nothing to do with the Royal Bastards anymore, but it's ingrained in me that I shouldn't be talking to another club unless they've been checked out and approved. "I need to get out," I add, waiting for Darren to move, but in true cocky biker style, he just leans back so I have to climb over him to get out.

I grab Bria and drag her a few steps away. She glares at me with irritation. "What's wrong with you?" she snaps.

"I'm not comfortable talking to—"

"Live a little," she cuts in. "Face it, Bully chose the club over you, Livvy. You wasted five years over that arse, so kick back and relax. Enjoy a night with your friends. I'm not saying marry this guy, but at least chat and remember what it was like before Bully came along and stole my sister." Her words make my heart ache, and I give a slight nod. Bria brushes my hair from my face and smiles. "Besides, they're fit."

I sit opposite Darren, and he gives me another award-winning smile. "You had a bad experience?" he asks. "With bikers," he adds to clarify.

"I don't really want to talk about it," I mutter, grabbing the sours and topping my glass.

"Suits me," he replies, grabbing a second glass and holding it up for a top-up. My phone buzzes again, and I snatch it from my bag, opening the text message.

Bully: Found you.

I frown, staring at the words before looking around frantically. If he sees me talking to another guy, let alone a biker, he'll end up right back in prison. I stand abruptly. "I have to go."

"But we've barely spoken," Darren says, his tone teasing.

Bria is nowhere to be seen, and I groan, typing out a text to tell her I left and to call me when she gets home. Lisa glances my way, and I reiterate the message to her. "Are you okay?" she asks with concern.

I nod. "Just tired," I lie. I don't want to drag them all away from their night out because of Bully.

I'm almost at the exit when a large hand slips around my wrist and tugs me to turn. Bully smirks, stepping so close, I have to tip my head back to look at him. His hand automatically slides around my throat in a loose hold, and I get that nervous, excited feeling in the pit of my stomach.

As if he senses it, he grips a little tighter and slowly drags his lips past my cheek and to my ear. "Told you I was coming." My heart slams hard, and my breaths quicken. Heat pools between my legs. "Your place or mine?" he asks.

"It's not a good—" *Idea* dies on my lips as he cups my cheek with his spare hand and kisses me until I'm breathless.

"Yeah, I heard all that before. But I ain't asking twice, Liv."

"The Marriott," I murmur, regretting it instantly. When Bria finds out about this, she's gonna gut me like a fish, but I don't stop myself from following him from the bar and out into the street.

I stare at our joined hands as he leads me through the crowds of party animals and towards the hotel I'd carefully picked over three months ago. When I could see an end in sight to his sentence. Everything seemed much less complicated back then.

His tattoos cover his hands and crawl up his arms, spanning across his back and chest. I've forgotten exactly how many he's got, but he added to them in prison.

His tattoos were the first thing I'd noticed when we met in a bar all those years ago. I'd found him outside after a fight, waiting for his brothers to come pick him up. I insisted on going to the hospital with him, and we were pretty inseparable after that . . . until he went inside.

The hotel is a few streets away, and as he leads me inside, the bright lights and twinkling chandeliers startle me into panic mode, and as if he senses it, he turns on me and presses me against a pillar by the reception desk. "Don't overthink it," he warns, his eyes burning into mine. "Forget all the shit. It's just me and you, here, alone. Me and you, darlin'."

I give a slight nod, and he relaxes, stepping back so I can approach the reception desk. "I have a room booked in the name of Bull."

The receptionist taps away on her computer before smiling and sliding a key card across to me. "Room three hundred and one, on the third floor."

I take the card and head for the lift with Bully right behind me. My mind races as we step inside and I press for the third floor. "You're doing it again," he says, slipping his arms around my waist and resting his chin on my head. I open my mouth to speak, but he places a hand over it and nuzzles against my neck. I close my eyes, enjoying the feel of his bristles against my skin. "I don't wanna talk," he tells me. "I haven't been in a room alone with you for five years, darlin'. The last thing I wanna do is talk." He takes his attention back to nipping my neck, and as we step from the lift, he keeps hold of me.

I press the card against the door and it opens.

Bully doesn't give me a chance to look around as he kicks the door closed and pushes me against it, kissing me hard.

Bully

Feeling her body pressed against mine compares to nothing else. It just feels right. My hands travel up her thighs and under her skirt, where I hook my thumbs into her knickers and drag them down her legs, kneeling before her while she steps from them. I stuff them in my pocket and smile up at her. She watches cautiously as I push her skirt to her waist and press my nose between her legs. I've spent years trying to remember this exact scent. *Her scent.*

My hands cup her peachy backside. It's fuller than I remember, *sexier*. Her legs part as I move closer, dragging my tongue through her folds and tasting her. I close my eyes, savouring her taste before pressing my mouth back there and licking her. She shudders, the sounds of her breathy moans spurring me on.

Liv's fingers run through my hair, gripping it at the roots and pulling my mouth closer as she lifts one leg and hangs it over my shoulder. She grinds her pussy against my face, and I lap her juices faster as she shivers through an orgasm.

Her breathless pants fill the silence as I rise to my feet and unbuckle my jeans. She eyes me warily, and I can see doubt creeping in. I shake my head cos there's no fucking way we're going over that break-up bullshit she spouted earlier. I kiss her, groaning at the thought of her tasting herself on my tongue. "We waited far too long," I murmur against her lips as I grip her legs and lift her against the door. My cock presses at her entrance, and she grips my shoulders as I ease into her. "Fuck," I pant, squeezing my eyes closed as she tightens around me. "You feel too good." There's no way I can control this as my body begins to move of its own accord, slamming into her at a punishing pace. She clings on for dear life, crying out with each thrust.

I turn us, moving away from the door and carrying her over to the bed, where I lay her down and continue the onslaught. "We're not over," I grit out, fisting her hair and pulling her mouth up to meet mine. "You're my old lady," I add. She remains quiet, her eyes avoiding mine as I take what I need. "Say it," I hiss, nipping the delicate skin of her neck.

"Bully," she whispers reluctantly.

"Say it," I demand, my tone more forceful. The rush of warmth fills me from head to toe, and I still, straining against her as I push in as deep as I can and release on a feral roar that rips my throat apart. "Holy shit," I pant, glancing down between us as I slowly withdraw. Her glistening juices mixed with mine keep me semi-hard as I slide back in, taking my time to come down from the high and dragging every ounce of pleasure from my orgasm.

I eventually pull from her and crawl down her body, kissing across her stomach as I settle between her legs and press my thumb to her opening, gathering our wetness and rubbing it over her swollen clit. She shudders, her body jerking.

"Bully, please," she whispers. I drag the wetness over her backside, my thumb gently teasing her puckered hole. She fidgets away, but I clamp a hand over her leg to hold her still. "We need to talk," she continues. I press my mouth to her clit, flicking it with my tongue while continuing to push my thumb to her forbidden hole. She groans as I manage to break through the resistance barrier, inserting the digit while sucking her clit. Her back arches off the bed as I stretch the hole. "You're not listening," she snaps as I crawl back up her body, curling her legs to her stomach and rolling her onto her side. I lie behind her, my cock straining to feel her tight arse take me in.

"I'm listening," I tell her, holding the head of my cock to the tight hole. "You're not."

"You haven't said anything," she says, stiffening as the head disappears inside. I gasp, trying to slow it down, needing to savour every second of this.

"See, you're not listening," I repeat. "I said we aren't splitting up. That you're my old lady." I lunge forward, and she cries out, grabbing a handful of the sheets as I force her to take my length.

I tug her skirt up and over her head, throwing it to the floor. Then, I unclip her bra and add it to the pile. Her arse grips me, squeezing me as I fuck her, this time taking my time. I run my hand over her stomach and cup her breast, teasing her nipple. "I can't compete with the club," she argues, and I laugh.

"I haven't asked you to."

"But it's expected," she snaps, turning her head into the mattress and groaning. I guide her onto her stomach and lie over her, my legs either side of hers as I move faster, fucking her into silence. I slip my hand under her stomach and slide it between her legs, using the wetness there to tease her clit. She shudders, her backside tightening as she comes apart. I follow seconds later, spilling into her.

I roll from her, our bodies slick with sweat, and I stare up at the ceiling, trying to regain control of my breathing. She sits, taking the sheet from beneath her and wrapping it around her body. "It's me or the club, Bully," she mutters, sliding from the bed and heading for the en-suite.

CHAPTER FOUR

Olivia

I half expect him to be gone when I return freshly showered, so when I find him sitting up in bed watching television, I'm surprised. I gave him a clear out, and I expected him to take it.

"I missed a good mattress," he tells me, "and a homecooked meal." He flicks the quilt back and gives me a pointed stare, waiting for me to climb into bed. Truth is, I want to, like *really* want to, but there's a voice in the back of my head screaming at me to stick to my guns on this. It's non-negotiable.

"Actually, I'm gonna head home," I say, the words almost clogging my throat.

"No, you're not," he says clearly. "Get into bed."

"No," I snap. "This isn't happening."

He scoffs. "The sex that's already happened?" He sighs. "Why are you fighting this, Liv? Bria's finally got into your head."

"No," I cry in frustration. "This isn't Bria. It's me talking, Bully, and you just refuse to listen. You promised me the club was behind us."

"I didn't," he says, shaking his head. "I never promised that."

"You said you'd get out of prison and make a life with me."

"But I never said I'd turn my back on the club."

"It was implied," I hiss. "You know how I feel about it."

He scrubs a hand over his beard and sighs heavily. "Get into bed, Liv."

"I'm leaving," I repeat, snatching my skirt from the floor.

"I can't let that happen."

"You don't have a say anymore. I met someone tonight," I say, tugging my top on. His stare is pure rage, and I resist the urge to run. "It made me realise there're men out there who would put me first." I hate the jealous glint in his eye, but I didn't tell him to piss him off. I need him to see I'm serious about this.

"I'm gonna pretend you didn't just tell me that little piece of infor- mation, Olivia." *Full name equals serious.* "Get into bed."

I stuff my bra into my bag. "And that's the sort of man I deserve," I continue. "You have your club, and I get you love it, but there's no room in your life for both of us." I turn on my heel and march for the door. I almost reach it when I'm slammed against it, trapped between that and his hard body.

"You're wrong," he whispers, wrapping his strong arms around me. "I can keep both. Just give me a chance."

"And when you end up back inside?" I ask, my voice wavering with emotion. "Do I spend another five years waiting around?"

"I won't go back inside."

"If they rang you now, would you leave?" I feel him tense, and any sign of hope slips away. "Exactly. Just let me go, Bully. I'm making this easier for you." He walks me backwards, farther away from the door, with his arms still firmly wrapped around me.

"One night," he mutters, sitting on the bed and pulling me onto his lap. "We'll talk tomorrow."

He slides back, leaving me sitting on the edge, and as he lies down, he takes my hand and tugs me to lie beside him. "Please, Liv."

I never could resist his pleas, so I lie back and allow him to wrap himself around me. I've spent so many nights thinking about this moment, making it all the more bittersweet.

I wake with a start, untangling myself from Bully's limbs that seem to be holding me hostage. I grab my bag from the floor beside the bed and pull out my mobile. There's a text message from Bria.

> **Bria: I'm home safe and sound. I'll call round for breakfast. Love you xx**

I groan, noting it's almost ten a.m. "Shit," I mutter.

Bully stirs, reaching for me and dragging me closer. His eyes remain closed as he seeks out my nipple, sucking it gently into his warm mouth and setting my insides on fire. "This is how I want to wake up every day," he mutters, his voice gruff from sleep. He climbs over me, settling between my legs and easing his erection into me. *Why am I so fucking weak for this man?*

We make love. It's slow and silent, just the occasional breathy sigh as we both reach an orgasm. And then he slips from the bed and heads for the bathroom. "We can grab breakfast," he calls out as he turns the shower on.

"Great," I reply, finding my clothes screwed up at the end of the bed. I pull them on. I glance around, looking frantically for my knickers, but they're nowhere to be seen.

"Is that pancake place still open in the centre of town?" he asks.

"Erm, I think so," I reply, picking up my heels and checking the room one last time for anything I've left. Then I head for the door, carefully opening it and trying not to make a sound as I slip out and close it equally as quietly. Then I make a run for the stairs, knowing it'll be quicker than the lift.

The perks of having an apartment just on the city centre's outskirts is it's cheap to get around. It takes me ten minutes to walk the distance from the hotel to my place, and I sigh in relief when I step into the foyer to greet the security guy. He gives a stiff nod as I pass and head for the lift.

"You dirty stop out." I spin to find Bria holding two takeout cups and a paper bag. I snatch that first and open it as I step into the lift. Inhaling the scent of breakfast rolls, I smile in appreciation.

"You're one to talk. Four a.m. you text me. Don't tell me you were clubbing until then."

She gives a slight smirk, dipping her hand into the bag and retrieving a bacon roll. She takes a large bite. "You go first."

"No, please, you totally have that mischievous glint in your eye."

The lift opens on my floor, and we step out into the corridor. I place the paper bag between my teeth and rummage in my handbag for my keys, letting us into the apartment. I kick off my heels and drop the keys in the dish by the door. Bria follows me into the open-plan living area and places the coffees on the worktop. "He was hot. Single.

Covered in tatts and a total shit kisser." I burst into laughter, and she arches a brow. "He was the type to think about himself. He probably wouldn't even get a finger wet." I laugh harder. "So, please tell me you had the best night."

I sip my coffee. "Well, he was hot. Strong. Covered in tattoos. A god in the sack—"

"Oh Jesus, Livvy, you didn't," she cries.

I bury my head in my hands and release a long groan. "Why can't he be shit in bed with a small dick?"

"I can't believe you gave in to him so easily. I knew I shouldn't have left you alone."

I look up and point a finger at her. "Exactly. This is all your fault. Your stupid plan to find me a man backfired, and I walked right into Bully's open arms." I take my roll from the paper bag. "Did you realise the men you hunted down were also bikers?"

She scrunches her nose. "Oh god, no wonder he was a shit kisser."

"He wasn't even good-looking."

"Well, I tried to hit on the one I gave you, but he wasn't interested. He asked me for your number."

I feel myself blushing. "He did?"

"Yep. And, of course, I gave it him. You're welcome."

I stare wide-eyed. "You didn't," I gasp.

"Did you see him, Livvy? Of course, I did. Had I known he was a biker, I would've rethought that."

I groan. "Now what do I do?"

"It's going to be pretty hard to convince Bully you're done when you let him give you orgasms." She eyes me suspiciously. "How many did he give you?"

"Last night or this morning?" I ask, almost smirking.

She cries out dramatically. "I hate you," she says, her tone teasing.

My smile fades. "Well, now we're not together, maybe you can jump his bones." The words make me feel sick, and she scowls.

"Gross. He was like my brother."

"I ran out on him," I admit, and she winces. "I just left the hotel while he took a shower. He's gonna lose his mind."

"And here we are again," she mutters, pushing the last bit of her roll away. "You do this shitty dance with him every time, and we all know where it ends—with you and Bully together."

"We had five years of peace," I say sadly. "It was nice."

"Maybe it could work," she says with a shrug, and I stare wide-eyed. She's the last person I expected to be championing our dysfunctional relationship. "You're in a better position this time around. You have your own place and a job. Before, you only had him."

"How long until he ruins it all, though? He'll get me fired from my job, and then I'll lose this place. Wherever he goes, there's a path of destruction, all caused by him demanding what he wants."

"So, don't let him stomp all over you," she says. "You hold the power here, Livvy."

Bully

Taz smirks as he sits back on the wall, watching me polish his bike. "You broke your own order," he chuckles, shaking his head.

An entire fucking week of polishing. *Why did I say that?* "I was trying to save my relationship," I snap.

"It's your rule, Pres. You can break it."

I add more polish. "No. My word is final. I should've been on time."

"Did you sort it with Liv?"

I shake my head. "I thought I was getting somewhere, but turns out, I was wrong."

"Are you giving up?"

I scoff. "No fucking way. She belongs with me." Her words from last night haunt me, and I sigh. "Actually, can you get Whizz to pull the cameras from Tudor's last night. She mentioned a guy."

He frowns. "She's met someone? That's impossible. We've kept a close eye on her. Pres, she's lived like a nun for the entire five years."

"Still, get him to pull the CCTV for my peace of mind."

Taz rescheduled church after my no-show this morning, so as the men gather for a second time, I wait patiently.

Once they're seated, I bang the gavel on the table to signify the start, and everyone quiets down and looks my way.

"I've got a call later this week with Jameson," I tell them. "How the fuck am I gonna tell him that the fucking Scorpions have slipped past my men and begun to build their empire right under our fucking noses?" They shift uncomfortably. "I want names, I want places, and most of all, I want some good news to take back to Jameson."

"We should reach out to our brothers farther south," adds Taz. "They might know names and history."

"Smiler, ask around the locals. Find me something." He nods. "I'll call Mouth from the Liverpool chapter." I look around. "The rest of you, keep your ears to the ground. This place ain't big enough for all of us."

Poison catches me as we leave church. "I made up your new room," she says.

I frown. "New room?"

"President always gets the top floor."

I groan. I hadn't even thought about that. It's huge up there, with a living space and bedroom. "I don't need all that room," I say.

She shrugs. "I don't make the rules, you do." And she struts off.

"You seem more relaxed," says Ragnar, throwing his arm around my neck. "Did you catch up with Liv?"

"You watched her, right?" I ask. "Did she ever meet anyone, a man?"

"No, Pres. I would've told you." I nod, but the feeling in the pit of my stomach is lingering. "Do you need me to keep watching her?"

"Nah, I can take over."

"You're the President now," he says, looking amused. "You have men to do the boring shit."

I arch a brow. "You're saying watching my old lady is boring?"

He backs away. "No offence meant, Pres."

I head for the office and notice the new chair sitting behind the desk. I smile as I lower into it, glancing at the worn chair in the corner. "I feel like you're still lingering, Hawk," I say out loud. "I've got it from here, Pres."

I pick up the phone and reach into the drawer for my dad's old notebook. It contains the telephone numbers for every single club member in the Royal Bastards. I used to laugh at him, telling him that mobile phones were much simpler. But using it, and holding his old office phone, makes me feel like I'm doing something right, so I find Mouth and dial the number.

"What?" he answers.

"Who pissed on your cornflakes?" I ask, laughing.

"Bully?" he guesses. "Shit, brother, I forgot about your release. I'm so sorry."

I laugh again. "Don't worry. That's not why I'm calling."

"I was gutted to hear about Hawk too."

"He left us without filling me in on a few things," I explain. "Seems the Bloody Scorpions have moved into my area."

"Those fuckers," he spits. "They're like poison seeping into the cracks."

"Yeah, tell me about it. I know fuck all about them, brother, or why they're suddenly here on our patch."

"I haven't heard shit, but if there's one thing I know about them, they like to pop up where they see opportunity. With Hawk going suddenly, that could be why."

"That's a good point. Cheers, Mouth."

"Yah know, you and that old lady of yours should come and stay. Genevieve would love to see Olivia again."

"I'll speak to her about it, and we'll sort a date. Thanks, Mouth."

"Anytime. Let me know if you need us, brother. We're always up for any opportunity to piss all over those fuckers."

I laugh before disconnecting. *Hopefully, it won't come to that.*

Taz enters the office holding up a memory stick. "Whizz got the CCTV from Tudor's, Pres."

He hands it to me, and I immediately plug it into my laptop. "Mouth made a good point," I tell him while I wait for it to load. "He reckons the Scorpions came here cos of Hawk dying. Maybe they didn't expect me to be out of prison?"

He nods thoughtfully. "You got ten years. They probably thought you were inside for another couple years yet."

"We need to show we're not weak. Get Boss to sort out a ride. Make it a charity thing so we get some coverage." He nods and heads out.

I take my attention back to the screen while bringing up Liv's details on my mobile phone. I press call and put it on loudspeaker.

The screen flickers through cameras. I select the one that overlooks the entrance just as the call connects. "Bully, I'm busy. I'll call you back." I like that she remembers how persistent I am when she ignores my calls.

"You left without saying goodbye."

"Yeah, well, I knew you wouldn't have let me go otherwise."

I spot her arriving on the camera and zoom in. She arrived with her friends, no men in sight. I flick on the camera that covers the bar, watching as she orders her drinks.

"We can't go back to how shit used to be, Liv."

I hear some rustling and then a door open and close. "I agree," she eventually mutters.

"Are you free for lunch?"

"Today?" I note a slight rise in her voice and frown. "Erm, no, I can't make it today."

"Then dinner tonight?"

"Bully, you don't do dinner," she says, sounding exasperated. "You don't do dates."

The next camera only just catches the booth she was sitting at, but she's out of my view. I notice Bria going off, leaving the rest at the table. "I just told you, things need to change. Starting with making more time for you."

She sighs heavily. "Tomorrow?"

"It has to be today," I say firmly. I don't want to give her time to overthink. "Where are you, anyway?"

"While you were away serving time for your precious club, I was making a life."

"I know about that," I say, narrowing my eyes when Bria returns to the table with a group of men, none of which I can make out.

"I have friends to see, and a job."

"Stop pretending like we didn't talk every week, Liv," I snap. "I know about your friends. I know how much you love working at that damn dog sanctuary."

"Then you'll also know that Saturdays are my busiest day."

"Liv, I just got out of prison. Surely, you can make time to see me at lunch. They give you a break, right?"

She scoffs. "Are you shitting me? After what you pulled yesterday? Why is it that when I want to see you, you don't give me a second thought, but when you want to see me, I have to drop everything?"

I briefly close my eyes. "You're right," I mutter. "I'm sorry. I just want to make things good between us."

"Then start by listening to me and hearing what I'm saying. I can do tomorrow."

"Fine. Tomorrow it is."

"Great. I'll text you where to meet."

"Actually, I thought I could come over and see your place."

"You're doing it again," she snaps. "I'll text you."

I disconnect, groaning out loud in frustration. I can't make anything out on the CCTV, its images are too grainy. But I can make out her leaving alone, which I already knew seeing as she crashed right into me.

CHAPTER FIVE

Olivia

"I'm going on lunch," calls Ann, my boss. She hired me exactly five years ago, when I decided I needed to rely less on the club and make a life for myself and Bully. From the second I met her, we hit it off. Her love for all animals, not just dogs, matches my own, and the second she let me wander around the rehoming unit and she saw how much I loved the dogs, she offered me the job.

Our aim is to rehome every single dog we take, and we're good at it. "There's a guy coming in any time," she says, turning the appointment book towards me. "He only called half an hour ago, said he wanted to rehome an older dog." We exchange an excited look. It's not often we get someone looking for the older dogs. Everyone wants a puppy these days. "Exactly," she says with a smile. "That's why I got him straight in."

I laugh. "Okay, go, I'll be fine." She heads for the door. "Be back before one. I have a lunch date, remember."

"Promise," she calls back.

It took all my courage to pick up the call I got this morning from an unknown number. Bria pushed me into it, knowing it would be last night's guy. She then proceeded to listen in on the call, pinching me when I tried to get out of lunch. And even though I'm not looking for anything, and I seriously am not ready to move on, I know she's right. I have to start moving forward and leaving Bully behind. Besides, as she pointed out, it takes some balls to call over texting, and I liked that he put in the effort.

The door opens, and I glance up. My heart stops beating as Bully saunters over with that stupid cheeky grin in place. "What are you doing here?" I ask briskly, pushing to stand. The guy is seriously pissing me off with his selective hearing.

"I booked an appointment," he says, holding up his hands.

I scrub my hands over my face. "Jesus, Bully. Give me a fucking break." When I look at him again, his expression has changed to sadness, piercing my heart.

"I want a dog. I thought this would be the best place to come."

"You've never wanted a dog and now suddenly you do?"

"How do you know I didn't want a dog?" he asks, frowning. "When did you ever ask me that question?"

I press my lips together in a fine line. "You're not suitable."

"You've not done the assessment." I arch a brow, and he smirks. "The woman on the phone said you have to do one."

I groan in annoyance as I snatch a clipboard off the side and thrust it towards him. "Fill this out," I snap, and he takes it. I practically chuck a pen in his direction, and he catches it then takes a seat and begins to fill in the paperwork.

I sit back behind the desk, staring at my computer even though my mind is full of him. Just like always. *How am I supposed to concentrate when he's sitting right across from me looking fine?*

"Where's the jacket?" I ask, noting he's missing his leather kutte.

"I thought my colours might give your boss the wrong impression." It seems like such a small thing, but it's a huge gesture. He'd usually not take his kutte off for anyone. I bite my lip to stop the small smile as I pretend to tap away on the keyboard like I'm busy.

Ten minutes later, he approaches the desk and places the board down. "All done."

I take it and glance at his answers. "I don't think we have anything to match you," I say, shrugging. "But if we get anything, I'll call you."

"Maybe I can speak to the woman I talked to on the phone?" he asks, arching a brow.

"Look, we both know you don't want a dog and you turned up here just to see me. I'm not going to give you a dog because I know you're here for all the wrong reasons."

His scowl deepens. "Yah know, Liv," he mutters, leaning closer and fixing me with a penetrating look, "not everything is about you."

I lean back, crossing my arms. "So, you really want a dog?"

"I *really* do."

I sigh. "Fine. Follow me."

I drop the latch on the front door then lead Bully through to the kennels out back. The dogs immediately become restless, all rushing to the bars and barking. "We have three Staffordshire bull terriers," I tell him, "all over the age of six."

"What about that one?" he asks, stopping by Misty's kennel.

I stop too and smile. "Misty is a crossbreed, Chihuahua and something else. She's been here two years, since her owner died of old age. We think she's around nine herself." She holds a special place in my heart, and she's so sad here. I'd have taken her myself, but my building doesn't allow pets.

"I'll take her."

I frown. "She isn't a match," I argue.

"Let me in to say hello," he demands.

"She's quiet and withdrawn. She'll hate the clubhouse."

"Or she'll love it." I groan as I unlock her cage, and Bully slowly goes in, sitting on the floor. I wait, watching in surprise as Misty pushes to her feet and steps from her bed. She sniffs the air, and Bully holds out his hand. "That's it, old girl," he whispers. "Come and say hello." The dog moves towards him, and her tail begins to wag.

"You've got to be kidding," I mutter as she allows him to stroke her. "Don't you want a bigger dog . . . one that's more *you*?"

He scoops her up and holds her to his chest, letting her lick his face. "That's stereotyping," he says.

"I just know you and I know the club. A staffy would suit you."

"Misty is perfect," he confirms, standing.

"You want to take her now, like right now?"

"Is that okay? I don't want to walk away and make her think I didn't choose her."

My heart twists as I glance from Misty and back to him. "Fine. Whatever."

He follows me out to the front, and I get out Misty's file. He takes a seat while I run through everything, then he signs the paperwork. "Any donations are welcome," I tell him, passing him a card to scan. We always push for donations, even after our fees for each rehoming. They barely cover the vet bills.

"Have you had lunch?" he asks, sounding hopeful. "You could come to the clubhouse and help me settle her."

I run my fingers through Misty's soft hair, smiling as she snuggles against Bully's chest and closes her eyes. "I already told you, I have plans."

"With?"

"My friend." When he arches his brow, I add, "Female." I don't know why I choose to lie. Maybe it's to save the headache, or maybe it's because I desperately regret this morning's decision to have dinner with the guy. In fact, the minute Bully leaves, I'm going to cancel.

He steps close, and I tip my head back to look up. "I love you so much, Liv. More than you'll ever know. I just want a chance." My heart twists. *Doesn't he deserve a chance? Do I really want to give up everything?*

The knock on the door makes me jump, and I spin to see Ann waving. I laugh and head over to unlock it. "Sorry, I was out back for a minute, so I locked it."

"I also found this young man waiting around," she adds, glancing back. I freeze at the sight of last night's guy. "He's got a date with you," she adds, smirking mischievously. I feel my cheeks burning with embarrassment as he steps into the reception area. It suddenly feels too small, and my chest tightens as I glance back at Bully, who's glaring at me.

"It's not a . . . erm . . . it's not . . . oh god."

"What you're trying to say is, it ain't a fucking date because you're married," snaps Bully.

I gasp for breath, wincing. "I'm not married" is all I manage to spit out.

"Are you okay?" Ann asks, her face full of concern.

I shake my head frantically, my eyes wide, begging her to save me somehow. Darren looks just as concerned, and he steps closer, placing a hand on my arm. I let out a squeak, but it's not enough warning for the force that is Bully, who shoves him back.

I'm mortified, but the guy doesn't look at all put out. Instead, he smirks, straightening his shirt and squaring his shoulders like he's ready to fight.

"No," I shout, stepping in front of Bully, who's still holding Misty under his arm. "Just leave."

His eyes fall to me. "What?"

"Please, just go."

"You're not fucking going on a date with another man," he roars, and Misty growls like she's backing him up. Like she's suddenly found her strength. *Traitor.*

"I know," I say, and I glance at the guy. "I meant to call, but time got away from me. I can't make it. I'm sorry to mess you around, Darren."

He gives a slight nod. "Okay. Call me."

"She ain't calling you," Bully yells. Darren gives another smirk before leaving. *"Prick,"* Bully mutters under his breath.

Ann gives a sheepish grin. "I'll be out back," she mutters, rushing off.

"Well," I mutter, "that was awkward."

"I can't believe you." Shame washes over me. "You jumped out of my bed and made plans to go on a date?"

"It wasn't like that."

"You've changed."

His words hurt, and I fight my tears. "How dare you, after everything you've done to me," I cry. "You cheated and stayed in my bed the entire time."

He rolls his eyes. "Get over it, Olivia. It was years ago." I watch as he heads for the door. "I'm so fucking sick of apologising for that."

"Where are you going?"

"To settle my new dog in," he snaps, pulling the door open.

"I thought you wanted to talk?"

"I don't have the words right now," he mutters, leaving.

Bully

Turns out Misty is a natural on the bike. The second I put my kutte on and stuck her inside, she snuggled down with just her head poking out. And she stayed still the entire ride.

I pull up outside the clubhouse and get off the bike, unzipping the jacket and placing Misty on the ground. She immediately finds a spot to pee before following me inside.

Taz looks at her. "Pres, there's a rat following you."

"She ain't a rat. This is Misty, the new club dog."

"Most presidents find club whores, but you bring us *this*?"

I grin. "She'll be more faithful, and you've got less chance of catching anything."

He raises his eyebrows. "I dunno about that. She looks a little . . . worn."

"Get one of the prospects. I have a list of shit this thing needs."

Sparrow, our newest prospect, knocks on my office door, and Misty barks to alert me. She's fitting in just fine. "VP said you need some stuff picked up for a rat?"

I laugh. "Meet Misty." He crouches down, and she rushes to him for a fuss. "You like dogs?"

"I grew up around them," he tells me.

"Perfect. Here's some cash. Go grab me everything I need to keep it alive." I chuck a roll of notes on the desk.

Boss enters as Sparrow leaves. "The ride out is this afternoon," he tells me, placing a piece of paper on my desk. I take it and look at the route. "Right past the Scorpion's new clubhouse."

I grin. "How'd you get the location?"

"Not hard," he says with a shrug. "I called the hospital to arrange a toy donation for the sick kids. They asked if I was the bikers from the warehouse on Main Street. I had a ride in the area and spotted an old nightclub. It closed down years ago. Bikes all outside, they're not hiding."

"Perfect. Is the word out on social media?"

He nods. "Local news might even make an appearance."

"Have Brains come up with a little speech in case. I don't wanna talk to anyone."

It's almost three o'clock when we ride out of the club gates. Boss is the perfect man for Road Captain, always managing to pull off this shit at the last minute, and as we fall into formation, cars make way for us to pass through.

We ride all the way to the hospital without a hitch. Then, we spend some time passing out the toys and books that the prospects spent all morning buying. We chat to the staff about funding cuts, and Tally promises to look over our figures to see where we can help with donations. And then we head back, taking the route through Main Street. I slow right down, revving as we pass, and as the Scorpions step out, I lock eyes with the guy from earlier. He gives me the same smirk that almost lost him his face, letting me know that he knows exactly who I am and exactly who Olivia is to me. *Fuck.*

By the time we pull back into the club's car park, I'm seething. Taz jumps off his bike as I pace, throwing his helmet onto his seat. "What's wrong?"

"He's the guy," I yell. "Of course, he is."

I'm making no sense, so he shrugs. "What guy?"

The other brothers are coming over, all looking concerned. They probably heard me cursing the entire way back.

"He's sniffing round Liv," I say, running my hands through my hair. "He's trying to take my old lady."

"Pres, she ain't on the market," says Taz, giving an unsure laugh.

"She thinks she is," I mutter. "I stopped her going on a date with him earlier."

"Shit."

"Darren," I repeat.

"Or Dagger, as he's known," cuts in Ragnar. "He's the president."

"Fuckkkkk," I cry, gripping my hair by the roots and tugging. "He wants a war. He's openly asking for one."

"Then we'll give him one," says Taz with confidence.

"I just got out," I snap. "My probation ain't even over."

"Don't worry, Pres," says Ragnar. "We got you."

"We can't go into this blind," I snap. "We need a plan. And I need to know every single biker in their chapter. Jameson will want to know too. Let's get ahead of the game."

We head inside, and Birdy stops me in my tracks, her lips painted red and her heels clicking across the floor. I scan her lace-clad body and give my head a shake. I *can't* go there.

"Pres, Misty is such a cutie," she says, holding the mutt against her ample chest.

"The Pres needs a drink," snaps Taz, and she puts Misty on the floor and rushes behind the bar to get me a shot. I take the offered absinthe and drink it in one.

"If you need to unwind," she offers, pouring me a second.

"What you offering?" I ask, knocking it back.

"Whatever you need, Pres," she whispers seductively. "Everything is on the table."

"Pity I'm spoken for," I say, pushing off the bar. "Everyone in church," I bellow.

CHAPTER SIX

Olivia

I paint the gloss over my lips and take one last look in the mirror before turning to Bria, who nods in approval. "You look amazing. Are you hoping to meet a certain man out tonight?"

I scoff. "I'm *done* with men. Bully hasn't called all week. I think he's finally seen it."

"Seen what?"

"What I've been saying from the start, that we're not going to work."

"Or maybe he's sulking because of the whole lunch date thing."

His face flashes in my mind, tight with hurt, and I sigh. "I don't blame him," I murmur. "I lied to him."

"He's done worse," she deadpans.

"I *said* that, and he looked at me like I was some nagging housewife." The twist in my chest returns, familiar and sharp. "This is the longest we've gone without speaking since we got together."

"Exactly why a night out is perfect," she says, slipping back into her heels like she's armouring up.

"You think a night out is the answer to everything." I laugh, despite myself. "But, fine, you're not wrong. I need to feel normal for five minutes."

"Who knows, maybe you'll see the guy from last weekend."

"God, I hope not. He's been calling and texting like crazy, asking me out."

She frowns. "And you haven't said yes . . . *why* exactly?"

"Because Bully would murder him."

"I thought you said Mr. Hottie was a biker too?"

"He is."

"Then maybe *he'll* murder Bully."

I shake my head, a reluctant smile tugging at my lips. "I don't want *either* of them dead. Especially not over *me*. Can we just drop it? I'm not dating anyone. I've been on my own for five years. I'm good."

Stacy places the tray of shots on the table. "Did anyone hear about that fire?" she asks, sitting down.

"Why do we always start on shots?" I complain, taking one. "Why can't we be civilised and start with wine?"

"The fire on the High Street?" asks Laura, and Stacy nods.

"Apparently, it's a gang war or something."

"They always say that," Bria states, taking a shot too. "It was probably kids."

"So, why would they say it's gang-related?" asks Michelle.

"Because they don't want us to realise how bad kids are these days," Bria explains. "They'd rather you think we have gang members running around waging war against each other than thinking our little cherubs of society are thugs, hell-bent on causing chaos and destruction."

I laugh. "Coming from a teacher, that's pretty harsh."

"You think I'm joking, but they're animals. And don't get me started on the parents."

"What happened anyway?" I ask Stacy.

She shrugs. "This woman who comes in the chippy regularly said it was gangs. Some turf war."

"Please," laughs Bria. "Where are we, America?"

"Ladies." We all look up as Darren approaches, and I inwardly groan. "Nice to see you all again."

"Is this your regular?" asks Bria, looking amused.

"I was hoping to bump into your sister, actually. She's been avoiding me." His eyes penetrate into my soul, and I shift uncomfortably.

"I wasn't," I mutter feebly. "I was busy with work."

"Liar," singsongs Bria, and I glare at her for outing me.

"Maybe we could get a drink together now?" he asks hopefully, glancing back at the almost empty bar. "Just one?"

Bria grins, nudging me. I give a stiff nod, and his smile widens as I slide from the booth and follow him to the bar.

"What'll you have?" he asks.

"Lemon gin," I reply, and he places an order. We wait while the barman pours a gin for me and a beer for him, then he leads me to an empty table where I can still see the girls.

"So, what did I do?" he asks. I almost choke on my drink at his bluntness, and he grins. "I like honesty, Liv." I don't like how he says my name. *Just like Bully.*

"It's Olivia," I correct. "And you did nothing. I don't want to be a cliché, but it really is me and not you."

"And the guy at the shelter?"

I think over my words. "An ex . . . I guess."

"Husband?"

I shake my head. "Boyfriend. Long-term, but it's all very raw, I'd prefer not to talk about it."

"Relationships are hard," he says with a shrug. "They take a lot of work and understanding."

"Have you ever been married?"

He nods. "Yeah. She died. Well, actually, she killed herself."

I gasp. "I'm so sorry."

"Don't be. She struggled after she lost her job, and things got messy for a while. Sometimes, I think it was for the best." I inhale sharply at his careless words, and he laughs a little. "Sorry, that sounded way worse than I meant it. She was suffering, and sometimes when the suffering ends, it's a relief to everyone involved."

"Was it long ago?" I ask.

"Coming up to three years," he replies with a sad smile.

"You must miss her."

"So," he says, taking a breath and smiling, "seems we're both new to this."

Somehow, his words make me feel more relaxed. "I'm not looking for anything right now," I admit.

"But there's nothing to stop us just talking, right?"

I laugh. "Okay."

"What do you like to do, Olivia?"

I frown. It should be an easy thing to answer, but instead, my mouth opens and closes but no words come out.

"Let me guess, you forgot how to be you," he says, saving me from the awkwardness of lying.

I give a slight nod. "Is that pathetic?"

"Not at all. When you give yourself over to someone so freely, you lose yourself."

"I spent so long waiting . . ." I trail off, realising I've said too much.

"It's fine. You don't have to explain."

I take a breath. Why shouldn't I speak from the heart? After all, it's not like Bully wants to listen. "He was in prison," I confess, "and I waited."

"Wow. That's such a hard thing to do."

I like that he gets the magnitude of what I gave up for Bully. "Right."

"How long?"

"Five years." He gives a low whistle. "I put my life on hold for the first few months, and when I got used to him not being there, I forced myself to get a job and a place to live, things that had nothing to do with him. I think I always knew deep down that I'd need my own life to fall back on."

"So, he got out, and you broke up?"

I nod. "More my choice than his. I don't feel like he really appreciated how I'd waited. He got out and the first thing he did was go and see his stupid cl . . ." I trail off. "Sorry, you don't want to hear this."

"It's fine. You need to talk about it so you can move forward."

I smile. "You sound just like my sister."

"She speaks wise words."

"What about you? What do you like to do?"

He grins. "I like bikes. Always have. So, riding is my passion."

My heart sinks a little. "Are you in a club?"

"And animals," he adds, ignoring my question. "Mainly pigs."

I frown. "You like pigs?"

He laughs. "I grew up on a pig farm. Dad was a biker too, but he was also a good pig farmer."

"Wow, that sounds different."

"We lived out in the country."

Bria comes over. "I hate to interrupt, but I need to steal my sister for a quick minute," she says, grabbing my hand and dragging me a few steps away. "Taz called me. Bully knows you're talking to this guy. I think he's watching the bar or something." She glances around nervously.

"Taz called to warn you?" I scoff. It's not something he'd usually do.

"They're on their way. Apparently, this guy is bad news."

"Of course, he is. They'd say anything to ruin this." I go to walk back, but she takes my arm and tugs me back again.

"I'm serious, Livvy. You know I don't listen to what they say usually, but this guy is the president of a rival club in the area. It sounds serious."

I glance back to where Darren is watching us closely, and suddenly, I feel nervous. "What do I do to get away without raising suspicion?" I whisper. The last thing I need is a fight breaking out between the bikers.

"Tell him your kid woke up and the babysitter called." I laugh. "I'm serious, it'll scare him off."

My smile fades. "Is he really that bad?"

"Do you want to find out?"

I swallow the lump in my throat and go back, offering a weak smile. "I'm so sorry. The babysitter called, and my daughter woke up screaming for me."

He narrows his eyes in amusement. "Daughter?"

"Didn't I mention her?" He shakes his head. "She's three and a real drama queen. She'll never settle now."

"What's her name?" he asks.

"Erm . . ." My mind goes blank, and I stare at the bottle of beer. "Bud . . . e. Buddy."

He openly laughs. "Buddy?"

"Nickname," I mutter. "Sorry." I spin on my heel and scurry off to where the rest of the girls are waiting for me.

I breathe a sigh of relief the second we step out. "Jesus, you made me panic," I say accusingly at Bria. "He now thinks I have a three-year-old daughter called Buddy."

The women break out in fits of laughter. "Buddy? What the hell?" asks Bria.

"It was the first thing that came to mind. I'm not good at lying on the spot."

"Why did you tell him you had a daughter again?" asks Stacy.

"Because Bria told me to say it," I cry.

Bria gives an unapologetic shrug. "We all know men run a mile at the sniff of responsibility."

"It's a shame," I mutter, glancing back at the door longingly. "He was turning out to be quite nice."

The rumble of bikes fills the air, and I groan. "Great, now I'm going to get an earful from the man who's ghosted me all week."

They slow by the kerb, and Taz removes his helmet. "Get on," he barks in my direction.

I frown at his tone, waiting for Bully to remove his helmet, but he doesn't, instead remaining on his bike and staring straight ahead. "The rest of you get on anyone's bike," he adds.

I grab Bria, halting her from making a move towards them. "We're good, thanks."

Taz fixes me with a glare. "It ain't a request, Liv. Get on the fucking bike."

"I think we should," whispers Bria.

"I thought you hated them?" I hiss back.

"Yeah, but they seemed pretty worried about the guy back there. I want us to get home safe."

I roll my eyes. "Fine." I snatch the offered helmet from him and slip onto his bike, making sure to hold the bars at the back instead of his waist. I watch as Bria gets on behind Bully, wondering why he hasn't demanded I ride with him like he always used to. And it hurts. *The silent treatment hurts.*

Bully

I'm pissed. So pissed, my hands hurt from gripping the handlebars too tightly. I've spent the week watching from a distance, learning what she likes, what she does outside of work. I even asked what she'd ordered from her local takeout last night. The server thought I was a creep.

But I wanted to give her the space she clearly needed while I learned more about her, because even though I hate to admit it, she's right—I didn't listen as much as I should have on all those visits. I was too busy making sure no one was paying her any attention, letting my jealousy rule me.

But then Whizz tracked her phone to Tudor's and checked the live cameras to see her talking to that fucker, *again*, and I lost it. I can't even bear to look at her right now.

I blink, realising I drove the whole ride lost in thought and I'm back at the club. Taz pulls beside me, and Liv jumps off before he's even stopped the engine. She rips off the helmet and shoves it against his chest. "What the fuck am I doing here?" she demands.

Bria slides off from behind me, taking off her own helmet and passing it to me. "Calm down, Livvy," she soothes.

"Why are you suddenly complacent in all this?" she snaps.

Bria looks surprised at the anger aimed her way. "I'm not, but you're getting so upset. We can get a cab. The good thing is we're away from that guy."

I remove my helmet and get off the bike. "That guy who's part of The Bloody Scorpions," I say, putting my helmet away.

I head inside with the women hot on my heels. "Am I supposed to know who that is?" Liv demands.

"You're staying here," I say. "Both of you."

"I can't," Bria begins, and I spin, narrowing my eyes until she recoils.

"Both of you."

"Don't be ridiculous," Liv yells. "We have jobs and a life."

"And then you mixed yourself up in a war."

She follows me into the office, slamming the door closed. I sit, smiling when Misty jumps on my lap. Liv stands in front of the desk with her hands on her hips, looking around. "It hasn't changed." She says it like it leaves a bad taste in her mouth.

"You wanna decorate?" I snap. I open the drawer and pull out a roll of cash, throwing it on the table. "Then decorate, Liv. Whatever makes you happy."

"Why are you mad at me?" she snaps. "I'm the one who should be mad."

"You're always mad. Why change the habit of a lifetime?"

She glares at me then bursts into tears. My heart aches to hold her, but I grip the arms of the chair and force myself to stay seated. "You have this way of making me feel like a nagging old wife," she cries, swiping angrily at her tears. "Like my reactions are unjustified." I keep my mouth closed as she begins to pace. "I had everything planned, and you came out of prison and just continued in this life like you'd never left. I waited for you for five years, believing your promises to change your ways. Did you lie just so I'd stick around?"

"No," I say, frowning, "of course, I didn't."

"And the day you got released, I sat outside like a fucking idiot, Bully. I was excited to see you, to finally be able to hold you without being told off by a guard. I chose my outfit, my underwear . . . I even went and had my hair done. I booked us that room so we could spend the day and night uninterrupted."

"We stayed at the hotel," I argue.

"To fuck," she screams back, and Misty growls. "We fucked," she repeats more calmly.

"And you walked out the next day like we were a one-night stand. So, *you* made it seedy, not me."

"Because that's how it felt," she whispers sadly. "The only time you spend any time with me is when you're inside me."

"That's not true."

"Five years of visits, once a week. Daily phone calls for five minutes. What did you learn about me, Bully?"

I lower my eyes, knowing she's caught me out. "We're both adjusting," I mutter.

"Nothing," she says, rolling her eyes. "You learned nothing. And the years before that, you spent wrapped in this club. I know this is your life, Bully, and I've given up trying to make you notice me. So, let me go. Stop holding on to me when you have other priorities."

"So you can go and fuck the president of the Scorpions?" I spit. "You think he'll have more time for you than me?"

"He turned up there. I had no idea."

"But you sat and had a drink with him."

"I was being polite." She sighs. "I have no interest in him or his damn club. But one day, I will move on from you, Bully. Surely, you know that."

"Why can't you just stay by my side, support me with the club?"

"You know why."

"Because you blame them for me going inside?" She nods. I take a breath and look her in the eye. "I know you want to believe they made me do that shit," I tell her, "but you know me, Liv. You know it was me." She shakes her head again, this time breaking eye contact. "I beat him, and if I hadn't been stopped by Hawk, I'd have finished the job."

"No," she whispers.

"You know deep down and you're trying to find reasons to justify it. But you *know* this is me. I am *that* guy. I live on a very thin line between good and bad, and let's not pretend that's not the reason you fell for me in the first place."

"If you weren't loyal to this club—"

"I'd be inside for murder," I tell her. "This club gives me a reason to live. It keeps me on that line instead of letting me cross over and living my life on the dark side. Hawk didn't ask me to go after Pearce. I did that because it was the right thing to do. He didn't deserve to breathe after what he did to your sister, and I did what I did for that reason, not because the club ordered it or I wanted to prove myself."

"Bria wanted him to pay."

"And he did pay."

"By the proper channels," she screams. "She wanted justice."

I stand abruptly and round the desk, standing close so she has to crane her neck back to look at me. "I gave her that because he was gonna walk from prison, Liv."

"You don't know that."

I groan in annoyance. "He was gonna walk, I promise."

"The whole trial collapsed because of you."

I grip her shoulders, gently shaking her. "The judge was corrupt. He was going to walk free. I had to give him a clear message." She shakes her head and tears slip down her cheeks. "I want to protect you. I like that you don't see the darkness in this world, Liv. It's why I let you look at the world through innocent eyes. But I know different, and I am telling you to trust me on this. He was going to get off. Stop blaming the club. It was on me." I release her. "I think you were looking for any excuse to hate this place," I add, my tone gentler.

"If I hadn't been involved in this club, I never would have introduced Bria to that monster."

I nod in understanding. "And that's the real issue, *you* feel guilty," I mutter. "Why did you wait for me, Liv?"

She glances up. "Because I love you."

"If that's true, you wouldn't ask me to choose. You're looking for reasons. You know damn well I won't leave this club, and I don't think you even want that. You want a reason to walk away so you can tell everyone I wouldn't choose you. Deep down, you blame me, but you can't openly say that because everyone will tell you you're wrong. You'll look unreasonable, and we all know how you hate to be the one to blame for anything."

She glances away. "That's not true."

"We all lost out the day Bria got attacked," I snap. "I lost a brother, and Hawk lost a nephew. My dad lost a son. But we put you and Bria before the club." She opens her mouth to speak, but I don't give her a chance. "Not only because we loved you, but because it was the right thing to do. You both turned your backs, and I sat back and let that happen because I felt guilty. But I've had five long years to think shit over, Liv, and I realise it's not my fault. It's not the club's fault. It's not yours either. The blame is on him. Pearce. He did what he did, and he faced the consequences. And if I could, I'd kill him, but he even took that away from us."

CHAPTER SEVEN

Olivia

The moment Bria had set her eyes on Pearce, she'd fallen head over heels. He wasn't interested. He hadn't so much as glanced in her direction, and it turned out to be the topic of many of our conversations. The fact I was with his older brother made it easier for her to hang around and watch him through puppy dog eyes.

Pearce and Bully were brothers. Not like club brothers, but real blood-related. And they were inseparable. *Mostly.* I still remember the way Bria lit up the second Pearce asked her to go for a ride on his bike. It had been a weird day, with most of the bikers out on a secret run they couldn't tell us about. That wasn't unusual—club business was always private. But when they returned, something in the air felt off, like charged electricity bouncing around aimlessly.

I'd just assumed something had gone wrong and I left Bully alone. He always needed time to himself when he got like that.

I'd arrived home and gone straight to bed, not thinking too much about Bria because I knew she was in safe hands. Everything about the club felt safe and protective then.

It was the early hours when I heard her in the shower sobbing. I wasn't prepared for what I was about to find in there. She was standing under the water, and the entire bathroom was full of steam. Her skin was red raw from the heat, and I immediately turned it off, which brought her from whatever nightmare she was lost in. Her eyes found mine, and the pain shining in hers almost broke me there and then. Her hair was matted, sticking to her face, and I noticed bruises appearing right before my eyes. And her feet were dirty, like she'd run barefoot through the depths of hell.

I'd held her until she stopped sobbing, and it was only when she began to shiver from the cold that she stepped from the shower and allowed me to wrap her in her dressing gown.

Some of the details stick in my mind as fresh as the day I witnessed them. Others have faded over time.

"You're right," I admit, finally meeting Bully's eyes. "I do feel guilty. I do blame you, and I blame the club. And I've tried to move forward. Lord knows, Bria wants that. But all those bad memories, they originate from here, from being in this club."

"Yet Bria is coping just fine," he snaps, looking past me and through the office window. Bria is sitting at the bar, chatting with Lords, the club's Chaplain.

"On the outside, maybe."

"She's dealing with it better because she isn't blaming the club."

I roll my eyes, sighing heavily. "We're going around in circles, Bully."

"Talk to her. Ask her who she blames," he demands. "I know the club didn't deal with things in the right way at first, but in the end, we did what was right."

"You didn't believe her," I snap. "You sat on the fence."

"He was my brother."

"And she's my sister."

He runs his fingers through his hair. "Yah know, I don't get why we're still fighting over this. Pearce is dead and still causing me shit from beyond the grave."

"I want to take Bria home," I mutter.

"No. The club's on lockdown until further notice."

"I don't belong to the club, and Bria certainly doesn't."

"Dagger is going after you to get to me." When I frown, he sighs. "Darren. He's the president of the Scorpions."

"He never mentioned you. And how would he know about us?"

"Trust me, he knows. And until I know what his game is, you need to stay here."

I scoff. "Have you ever actually thought he might like me? Is the thought so abhorrent to you that a man could actually want to get to know me?"

He rolls his eyes. "Of course not, but these bikers have been a pain in the club's side since before I was born. The history is too much of a coincidence for me to ignore it."

I groan dramatically. "Fine. I want a room with Bria. I'm not leaving her alone with your men."

"Whatever," he mutters. "I'll have one of the whores sort it for you."

"I can sort my own room. I don't need your sex slaves running around after me." I stomp from the office and head for Bria, who looks surprisingly calm considering. "Let's go find a room."

She jumps off the stool. "We're staying?"

"If that's okay with you? He's being dramatic, thinking I'm in some kind of danger."

She slips her hand in mine. "Then that's good enough for me."

We take the stairs and go to the first floor. Guests usually stay here, and the rooms that are free have doors propped open. We take one with twin beds, and I go to the cupboard to find bedding. We make the beds in silence. I have a million things racing around my head, and eventually, she laughs, "Okay, out with it."

"Huh?"

"Your mind is working overtime. What's wrong?"

I sit down on my bed and cross my legs. "Bully said I'm projecting."

She laughs again. "That doesn't sound like a *you* thing," she says, her tone teasing.

"Don't tell me you agree with him."

"Depends what you're projecting about." When I don't answer, she sits on her bed facing me. "Pearce," she mutters in a low voice.

"How can you even say his name?" Her fingers interlace the way they always do when she's anxious. "Look, we don't have to talk about this," I add quickly.

"Why do you do that?" she asks. "Assume I don't want to talk about it, like it's some shameful secret."

I gasp. "Bria, that's not what I meant."

"You're just like Mum. It's why I moved out of there. I was raped, Livvy. I'm not ashamed. I did nothing wrong."

I jump up, joining her on her bed. "I know you didn't. I'm sorry if I'm getting it all wrong."

"We don't talk about it because you were sad that Bully went to prison. It all happened so fast. The trial, and then Bully getting arrested and charged . . . and then Pearce dying." She stares down into her lap. "And now, Bully's out and you're still sad."

Tears fill my eyes. "Oh god, I've made it about me."

"No," she's quick to say. "I just never brought it up because I didn't want to make things worse between you."

"I remember leaving the police station and taking you home," I say. "And once you'd fallen to sleep, I went to see Bully."

"I didn't know that," she says, frowning.

"I never told anyone. I was so upset with his reaction, I couldn't bring myself to tell you."

"When he didn't believe?"

I nod. "He dropped my hand like it was a hot poker, shaking his head and telling me I was wrong, that Pearce wouldn't do that." I wipe my tears, feeling shame wash over me. "I should've dumped him there and then. I didn't and I've spent years thinking about the way he reacted, resentment building inside me."

Bria takes my hands in hers and smiles sympathetically. "Pearce was his brother. He didn't want to believe what he was capable of, but in the end, he saw the truth."

"And then he ruined the trial."

She nods. "He did. And I was mad too. But things worked out. Pearce is dead. He can't hurt anyone else."

"But he didn't pay. Not really."

"He took a pretty good beating. The thought of spending life in a wheelchair was too much for him, so he took his own life. I call that a win."

"I'm so angry," I admit.

"At the wrong person."

"What? You're telling me you don't blame the club for everything?"

She shrugs. "I did, at first. Therapy helped me deal with it, and now, I can see it's only Pearce who's to blame. He's not here, so I have to let it go or it'll eat me alive. Besides, Bully is in charge now. Things might be different."

"I want a normal life. I want kids and a house."

"Can't you have all that with Bully?"

I shrug. "I guess I feel bad," I admit. "Shacking up with my sister's rapist's brother."

"He was your boyfriend before Pearce was my rapist." She offers a little smile. "For what it's worth, I think Bully does love you. He just needs to learn to treat you with the respect you deserve."

"Everything about him is wrong for me."

She grins. "But he feels so right?" I nod, and she laughs. "Then stop punishing yourself and him. Give him a chance to be what you need. He's had five years to grow up. You just have to get to know one another again."

Bully

I take my seat in church. "Smiler, tell me you have something."

He nods, smiling wide and showing his ear-to-ear scar. "Yes, Pres. Dagger was from the London faction of his club. He was the VP and then decided to start his own chapter here in Nottingham. He was married, but there's no record of her being here with him, so I didn't look into her. She seems irrelevant. His VP goes by the name Bullet, on account of his favourite murder weapon." He rolls his eyes. "The other members are OGs, no one younger than fifty by the looks of things. They're recruiting for prospects, so they want to expand. Their main income is drugs. I'm looking into storage units to see if they're shipping in or if they have grow farms around. Something tells me weed is too small-time for them, although the market is thriving in Nottingham."

"It's too saturated already," agrees Taz.

"Word on the streets is that spice is rife," Lords chips in. "I'm volunteering on the streets next week in the town centre. I'll get people talking."

Smiler pulls out his mobile and shows us the damage from the fire we started a few nights ago. "I got a guy in the fire service who sent me these."

I smirk. "I hear they're still in there though."

He nods. "Yep, the fire didn't touch upstairs. There's an entire floor they can live on."

"Good," I say. "I want them where I can see them. We'll wait, see if they retaliate."

"And when they do?" asks Ragnar.

"We'll be ready."

I'm heading out when Liv steps in front of me. "I want to talk," she says.

I inwardly groan. I'm so sick of arguing with her, and I really just want to get out of here for a quiet ride. I hold up the bike keys. "I'm riding out." Disappointment fills her expression, so I add, "You wanna come?" A smile pulls at her lips, and she nods, following me out.

I drive for half an hour. The sense of freedom it gives me instantly lifts my mood, and as I slow into a car park, I'm glad Liv came with.

I take her hand and lead her to the edge of the hill. It's the perfect spot to watch the sunset, a place I've been coming to since I was a kid. A place I vowed to bring Liv to while I was banged up inside.

"Wow," she whispers, taking it all in. "This is beautiful."

I lay out my jacket so she can sit on the grass, then I drop down beside her. "I've been thinking over our argument," I say.

"About that . . ."

"Let me say this," I tell her, "or I'll mess it all up again." She gives a nod. "I love you. It's always been you. And yeah, before, when we first met, I was an idiot and I thought I could have it all. Club whores threw themselves at me the second I became VP. I hurt you, over and over, but you stuck around. And I appreciate that. I'm done with other women and stupid games. I just want you, Liv."

"I spoke to Bria," she almost whispers. "She kind of agreed with you. I am holding on to some kind of anger and blame, but I know it's not our fault. I'm sorry."

I brush a hand over her cheek and cup her face. "The club is my life, Liv, but so are you. Don't tell me I can't have both. Please."

"We'll try," she says, and my heart swells. "I can't promise it'll work. But I will do my best to support you."

I slam my lips against her in a bruising kiss. "Thank you."

We stare out at the sinking sunset. "You were wrong before," I say, and I feel her look at me. "I do know things about you. You like vanilla ice cream with pecans. You drink decaf everything because caffeine makes your heart race and you hate the feeling. You like gin, lemon is your favourite, and if you could, you'd home a thousand dogs." I turn to her, and she's smiling. "You like hot baths and white roses. Chocolate with salty crisps," I grin, "at the same time."

"It's nice," she argues, laughing.

I climb onto my knees and lean forward so she has to lie back. I lift her top slightly and kiss her stomach. "You want children, two. You want to get married, but you don't want the traditional white wedding because you hate to be stared at." I glance up, and there's heat in her eyes. "You like to be on top, but you also like me to be in charge." I gently bite her nipple through her shirt, and she gasps. "You give the best blowjobs in the world." She laughs out loud. "And when you walk into a room, it lights up. I hate that men stare at you, but at the same time, I'm amazed you don't pay them any attention. I love you, Liv. I always have and I always will."

"I love you too," she replies, running her hands through my hair. "I'm sorry for everything."

I brush a finger over my name tattooed across her collarbone. "We belong together. You know that." I kiss her one last time before standing and holding out my hands for her. She grabs them, and I pull her to her feet. "Now, let's get back so I can get you naked."

CHAPTER EIGHT

Bully

I'm hot . . . too hot, and I throw the sheets back and sit, glancing down to see Liv curled up naked. I smile. It feels good to have her back on side, because even with the five years apart, things felt heavy.

I throw my legs over the edge and grab my jeans, tugging them on before heading for the door. It still feels weird being able to leave my room in the middle of the night, and I laugh to myself as I head downstairs.

Poison is in the kitchen, naked and downing a glass of water. She eyes me with a sexy grin as I pass her to turn the kettle on. "Can't sleep?" she purrs.

"Something like that," I utter, grabbing a mug. When I turn to grab the milk from the fridge, she's blocking my path. She grabs my hand and places it to her chest, closing her eyes in pleasure.

"I can help," she breathes. I try to free my hand, but she holds it tighter.

"If Liv catches you . . ."

She runs her free hand over my tattooed chest. "I'm discreet," she whispers, moving past me to grab her glass of water. She tilts the glass, allowing the water to trickle over her chest, and I follow it with my eyes as it drips from her nipple. She slides her hand around the back of my neck and tugs my head a little closer while pressing her lips to my ear. "Taste me," she whispers.

I pull back. "Stop," I snap.

"Oh, please, don't stop on my account." My head whips round to find Liv leaning in the doorway, and relief floods me, followed by panic.

"It's not what you think."

She rolls her eyes, pushing from the doorframe and crossing her arms over her chest. My shirt she's wearing rides up, and I eye it with jealousy. If the brothers were to walk in now, they'd see her ass cheeks at the very least. "What I think is you're allowing a club whore to touch what's mine."

A thrill races through me at her possessive words, and then it registers that Poison still has one hand wrapped around my neck. She's smirking like having Liv catch her isn't a problem. She clearly hasn't heard the stories about her.

I back away, holding my hands up with a slight smirk. "You're right. I'm sorry."

Poison looks my old lady up and down with a raised brow, and I inwardly wince at her foolishness because despite Liv being five-foot-five, and Poison standing at least five-eight, she's no pushover. "Are you seriously telling the Pres what to do?"

Liv gives a smile of her own, one that screams a warning that only I can read. "No, I'm telling my old man to stay clear of rubbish like you."

"Bitch, I know you didn't just trash talk me."

"Enough," I say warily, stepping between the pair. "Liv is my old lady, she makes the rules."

"You realise that every biker, including the President, has side women. It's how this works," says Poison, crossing her arms. "And I'll let this slide because I assume you're new to all this, but seriously, you need to adjust your attitude because only the President can decide who sucks his cock."

Liv's eyes fall to me, that rage smile still fixed in place like some demented clown. "She's right, baby. Only you get to decide."

Poison smiles like she's won and steps around me. "I'm glad you're seeing sense," she mutters, heading for the exit. "Shall I wait in your office, Pres? We can finish what we started."

Liv is still watching me, but I'm not fooled by her calm exterior. And when her hand dashes out, entangling Poison's hair, I groan. She drags her close so her mouth is pressed to Poison's ear. "Let me be very clear," she hisses. "You touch my man again, I will rip your cheap extensions out."

"Get the fuck off me," Poison screams, trying to free her hair from Liv's grip.

"I think she gets the message," I say on a sigh.

"No, baby, I don't think she does at all." Liv proceeds to drag her from the kitchen kicking and screaming.

I follow reluctantly because if I've learned anything about Liv, it's to let her ride this out without getting involved. If I try to intervene, she'll lose her mind. The prospect jumps up from the couch looking overly alert. "Everything okay?" he asks, taking in the scene before him.

I arch a brow. "Does it look fine to you, Sparrow?"

"Go get all the club whores down here," Liv demands.

Sparrow looks my way for permission, and I give a nod. He rushes off. "What's the plan here, Liv?" I ask, going behind the bar and retrieving a bottle of rum.

"Your bitch is crazy," screams Poison, twisting to try to hit Liv, who dodges it effortlessly.

"I don't work off a plan," says Liv, shoving Poison down until she's on her knees. "But if you want me to stick around, we're doing this shit my way."

I pour a rum and take a seat. "Seriously, you're just gonna let this happen?" yells Poison.

"What the fuck is this about?" Brains demands as he follows Stiletto down the stairs. I take in her naked body and smirk. A lot of brothers are gonna be pissed to have been interrupted.

Taz stomps down a second later. "This better be fucking good," he growls, dragging Birdy behind him. He pauses when he spots Liv and groans dramatically. "Fuck's sake," he complains under his breath. "Who set Liv off?"

Once all the whores are present, Liv takes centre stage, making sure to look each in the eye, one at a time. "From now on, you don't touch Bully. Not even if he asks you to." She's met with sniggers from the men and raised brows from the whores.

"No disrespect, Liv, but the Pres is a big boy, and he can do what the fuck he wants," says Taz. He grabs Birdy by the hand. "Now, if you're done with the tantrum, I was in the middle of something."

"I'm not finished," she yells, and I note some of the women startle at her harsh tone.

Taz looks at me. "Are you gonna say anything here?"

"Brother, she's laying down the rules. Give her the respect she deserves."

He rolls his eyes, turning back to Liv. "Ladies, you heard her, right?" The women nod. "Pres is off limits." They nod again, but I don't miss the smirks as they glance at one another. If anything, she's just set them a challenge.

Olivia

I release my tight grip on Poison's hair, practically shoving her away from me, and she scrambles away, following the rest of them upstairs. They won't listen. I'm not stupid, and I know how this life works. It's almost tradition to fuck the President, so he's their main target. But I'm not going to sit back and let it happen. I've heard all the stories about bikers having an old lady as well as a bit on the side. That won't be me.

I shift under the weight of Bully's stare as he sips his drink, eyes trained on me like he's waiting for me to run. I stand my ground. "I'm serious," I tell him.

"I know."

"I won't stand by and let it happen. You fuck around again, I am out."

"Okay."

"And if you try to stop me, I'll stick a knife in your heart. That will not be my life. I am not my mother."

He nods again. "Okay."

I turn to leave, smiling when he rushes after me, wrapping his arms around my waist and lifting me off the ground. He bustles me into his office, kicking the door closed and lifting my shirt. "Fuck, you're hot when you're jealous," he pants, running kisses along my neck.

"I'm also dangerous," I warn as he bends me over the desk and unfastens his jeans. "Let's not push me over the edge."

He enters me, growling as his intrusion stretches me. "You were made to be my old lady," he murmurs, pulling my arms behind my back and slamming into me.

I lift one leg onto the desk, groaning with pleasure when he sinks deeper. "Let's see if you still feel like that when I put in the rest of my rules."

⧫

"Was that me, or was there a frosty feel to the air as we walked through there?" asks Bria.

I pull my leg behind me to my backside and stretch my muscles. "I had to lay down the law," I tell her, changing legs. I hate running, but since Bria's attack, we've made sure to do it four times a week. It helps her to clear her head, and it makes me feel closer to her. "I found Poison dripping all over him last night."

I feel her eyes on me, probably asking herself the same questions I have. *Has he been there already?* "I can't think that way," I tell her without her saying the words. "I've decided to give us a chance, so I just have to get on with it."

"But we all know what bikers can be like—"

"Bria," I snap, tipping my head from side to side. "Yesterday, you were telling me to give him a chance, and now, you're questioning it?"

"I'm not," she argues, setting off, and I reluctantly follow. "But warning the whores off is like waving a red flag to a bull. They're gonna have competitions to bed him."

"What was I supposed to do, sit back and watch?"

She giggles. "No. Although, have you ever wondered what it would be like?"

I scowl. "To watch Bully fuck a whore?"

She shrugs. "To watch or be watched. Or even, yah know . . . join in."

I groan. "It's too early for this talk," I say, passing her and steaming off ahead.

Rabble is wheezing by the time we get back to the clubhouse. I watch with concern as he doubles over, gasping like he smokes eighty a day. I hand him my water, and he takes it gratefully. "What did you do to the prospect?" asks Boss as he steps out for his morning cigarette.

"Running isn't his thing," says Bria, grinning.

"You ain't gonna find a biker in there who loves a run," he says with a laugh as he lights up.

"You look pretty fit," says Bria, and I gasp at her brazen flirting.

Boss laughs some more, blowing out a plume of smoke. "Baby, I can fuck for hours. It keeps me fighting fit."

Bria blushes, and I continue to stare between the pair, feeling like I'm in the way. She loves a flirt and even a cheeky kiss on occasion, but she never takes it further. I don't blame her, but I doubt she'll ever trust a man again. "On that note, I'm gonna take a shower," she says coyly, heading inside.

Boss's attention falls to me. "You realise you set the whores a challenge last night?"

"I do," I say, shrugging. "But I've given them a warning. They hit on him, I start breaking fingers."

He grins. "I missed you. It was a mistake, you leaving like you did."

"Oh yeah, why's that?"

"You lost the respect of the men," he says casually.

I scoff, heading for the door. "You think that bothers me after what happened to my sister in this clubhouse?" He has the decency to look away. "I lost respect for the guys way before I left, Boss, so if you think this little conversation was an eye opener for me and I'm gonna break my back to try to win the guys over, you're wrong. If anything, it's you lot who need to impress me." And I saunter away. *Prick*.

I pause in Bully's office doorway as he tucks into a full English breakfast. It's weird seeing him sitting behind that big old desk, but strangely, it suits him. Maybe deep down, I always knew this was coming. It didn't stop me wanting him anyway. It still doesn't.

He glances up. "You okay?"

I nod, crossing my arms as I move closer. "You ever think about sharing me?"

He inhales, almost choking on a mouthful of bacon. "Huh?"

I shrug casually. "With another man . . . or woman?"

"What the fuck? Where is this coming from?"

"Bria mentioned something, and it got me thinking."

He rounds the desk, his face full of concern. We've always been adventurous in bed, but I've never even thought what it'd be like to share him. I shudder at the thought as he grabs my hands. "No, I haven't. Why the fuck would I share what's mine?"

I smirk, running my finger over his chest. "Maybe it'd be fun. Me. You." I glance around before adding, "One of your brothers."

His eyes narrow, and he shoves the door closed as he pulls me into his arms and kisses me. I begin to giggle, and he pulls back. "You're winding me up?" I nod, laughing as he lifts me into his arms, wrapping my legs around his waist. "You look good in Lycra," he whispers against my lips, "but get it off."

The tension is palpable, and wherever I go, club whores are whispering. I rise above it, ignoring them. They'll get used to things. I find

Bully about to go into church and pull him aside. "I want to invite my friends over."

He gives me that look that tells me he's about to object and come up with a ridiculous reason, so I kiss him until he can't breathe and smile. "Please."

"It's not a good idea. Outsiders make the brothers uneasy."

"Outsiders?" I repeat. "They're my friends, and if I'm going to be part of this club again, I want them around too."

"I'll run it by the guys."

I frown. "Aren't you in charge?"

He sighs. "It doesn't work like that. This is their home too, and they shouldn't feel uncomfortable."

"Fine. But if they agree, I want the whores out for the night."

He scoffs until I arch a brow to show I'm serious. His smirk fades. "They'll never allow that."

"Fine, I'll just go out then." I turn on my heel, ignoring him calling my name, and then I hear Taz asking to get church started. Bully disappears inside their unholy room. *Typical.*

I find Bria on her bed reading. She glances up then groans. "You have that look," she complains. "The one that tells me we're gonna get into trouble."

"He pisses me off," I cry in frustration. "And then I get the urge to do stupid shit."

"Like?"

"Sneak out of here and see the girls."

Bria grins. "They are out tonight. Lisa texted me."

I check my watch. "And the bikers will be busy for the next hour at least."

She throws her legs over the edge of the bed. "We better get a move on then."

CHAPTER NINE

Bully

Smiler takes the floor, clearing his throat before projecting a picture from his iPad onto the wall. "Fuck me, technology has advanced," mutters Tally. "Imagine Joker using this shit," he adds, shaking his head with a smirk.

"My dad wouldn't entertain a smartphone," I remind him, "so this would've blown his mind."

"Right, this is the floor we set fire to," Smiler says, pointing out the charred remains of the lower ground. "And now, they're living up here," he adds, pointing to the first and second floor. "Lords did some outreach work this past week," he continues, nodding to Lords, who stands.

"I was on the streets with the youth workers. I was right about spice being rife on the streets. Hospital admissions have risen by twenty percent since Dagger and his men have been on the scene. Arrests for public disorder from using spice have also risen."

"And there's no one else who could be pushing that shit?" I ask.

Smiler shakes his head. "No one else would dare, not without running it by the club. I've had feelers out all week, and it all points back to the Scorpions. Besides, no one else has the manpower to get that shit out so quickly apart from us."

"Are they using runners?" asks Taz.

"That's my next job, start shaking some dealers and see what we get."

"I want everyone on this," I cut in. "Take as many men as needed."

"It still doesn't answer the question as to why the fuck they've rolled up here," says Boss.

"I think Taz was right," I reply, rubbing a hand over my brow. "They saw an opportunity when Hawk died. Maybe they thought the club would drop into chaos with no leader." I glance to Taz and grin. "No offence."

"Some taken," he says, grinning back. "But they were wrong. You're here, and we need to make it clear they're not welcome."

"Smiler, come up with the plans to start banging on doors. I need to go and chase my old lady down before she goes AWOL." I head for the door.

"You need backup?" Taz quips.

I laugh as I head upstairs to the bedroom.

I pause in the doorway. The bed is littered with discarded clothes, and Liv's makeup is spread out on the dresser.

"Liv?" I call.

No answer.

I groan and head downstairs, praying she's in the bar. But when I find that empty too, a sharp bolt of panic spikes through my chest. I pull out my mobile and call her.

"Hey," she answers, light, breezy, like nothing's wrong.

"Hey yourself. Where are you, Liv?" My voice is tight.

"I told you, I'm out with the girls."

"You're supposed to be home." I try to keep my voice level, but the edge is already there. "You know what's going on with the Scorpions."

"I'm not a prisoner, and I'm not hiding just because some wankers are revving their engines," she says, casual as anything. I hear laughter in the background. Glasses clinking. A low beat from the music. The girls.

"Liv," her name comes out low, rough, "this isn't a joke. I told you to stay in for a reason."

"And I told you, I'm not being *that* woman. You think I'm safer holed up in the club with your men?"

"Safer than out there, yeah." I pace to the door, shoving it open and scanning the street like I might see her. "You have *any* idea what could go down tonight?"

"I have a right to live my life, not just sit in a box while you and your club handle everything your way. Before you got out, I did this all the time." There's steel in her voice now, but it's the wrong kind. Not fear, not defiance. *Challenge.*

I press my fingers to my temple, trying to breathe past the fury knotting in my gut. "Where. Are. You?"

"Don't you use that tone with me."

"I'm coming to get you."

"Don't you dare."

"Too late."

I hang up, already halfway to the bike. "Taz," I call, throwing my leg over the bike. He appears in seconds. "Liv's gone. I need to get her back here. Oversee Smiler's plan, and I'll join you soon as I'm done."

"You're not going alone," he says firmly, putting his fingers in his mouth and whistling loud enough to get the brothers' attention.

"Smiler, plan's on hold. We got an old lady to find," he calls over his shoulder as he heads for his bike.

Smiler and Boss rush out, and as I put my helmet on, I smile. I've missed the solidarity of my brothers.

Olivia

"There's a tracker on my phone," I tell Bria as we line up for the bathroom, "but I turned my phone off, so he shouldn't find me, right?"

"Right," she says, smirking.

"You think he will?"

"I think he knows all your tricks and he's probably one step ahead."

"Well, I don't care," I snap, pushing down the slight panic in my chest. "He's got to relax and realise I'm not in danger twenty-four-seven. Seriously, what can happen in a busy bar?"

A sharp, unnatural pop cracks through the noise of the bar.

We both freeze.

Then another pop, louder this time, and suddenly, the air shifts. Music cuts out. Screams erupt like an explosion. People shouting. *Panic.*

Bria grabs my hand, nails digging into my skin. "What the fuck is that?" she whispers, her face draining of colour.

Another pop. Then a shatter. Glass—maybe a bottle, maybe a window—crashes somewhere out front. The sounds come fast now . . . thudding boots, overturned chairs, more shouting. Angry voices. Male. Too many.

And then the bathroom door slams open so hard, it ricochets off the tiled wall.

Darren fills the doorway like a nightmare, face hard, eyes scanning, jaw tight.

"You need to move," he growls. He looks like violence, like barely restrained fury in a leather cut.

And for the first time tonight, I realise just how badly I've fucked up.

"What's . . . what's happening?" I ask, my voice trembling.

He closes the door, and suddenly, the room feels a hell of a lot smaller. He leans against it. "Get in the cubicle," he orders.

Bria drags me in, and Darren begins to pull it closed, his eyes reaching mine. There's a hint of something . . . *guilt* maybe? "Don't come out, no matter what."

"Why? I don't understand."

He goes to leave, and I reach out without thinking, grabbing onto his wrist. He pauses, staring at where we touch for a second before raising his eyes to mine again. "You might get hurt," I whisper.

A smile pulls at his lips. "Don't worry about me, beautiful. But if you want to see tomorrow, you can't come out of here until the police come. Got me?" I nod, and he rubs a thumb over my cheek, smiling. "Good girl."

Once he's gone, I close the cubicle door and turn to Bria. "What the fuck's going on?" I whisper, taking my phone from my back pocket.

"I'm still tripping on the good girl comment," she says, practically swooning.

I scowl. "Bria, focus."

She fans her face. "Sorry."

Bully

I jump off the bike, boots hitting the pavement hard, and take in the chaos around me. The bar is taped off and flashing blue lights paint the night in warning. Police everywhere.

"Jesus," mutters Taz as he pulls up beside me. "What the fuck happened?"

I'm already moving. Fast. Straight toward the tape.

An officer steps in my path, arm out. "You can't go in there."

"My wife might be in there," I snap, louder than I mean to.

"We're still getting people out. Be patient."

"*Patient?*" I growl, jaw locked tight. "What the fuck happened?"

Before I can shove past him, Smiler grips my arm, pulling me back just enough to stop me doing something stupid. "Relax," he murmurs in my ear. "Boss is on it. He's making calls now."

Then I hear it.

"*Bully?*"

Her voice cuts through everything—the noise, the panic, the adrenaline. I spin just in time to catch Liv as she barrels into me, arms and legs wrapping around me like she's never letting go. I bury my face in her hair, breathing her in.

"You had me fucking worried," I mutter against her temple.

I open my eyes and clock Bria standing nearby, pale but smirking, and a couple other women behind her looking sheepish. I lower Liv slowly to the ground, keeping my hands on her shoulders, scanning her for blood, bruises, *anything*. She looks fine, uninjured.

"What the fuck do you think you were doing?" I snap. She flinches, and my heart cracks, but the fear, the fury, they're boiling over. "This is why I told you to stay at the clubhouse."

She straightens, her shoulders squaring, her chin jutting out slightly. "I'm *fine*."

"Pres," Boss calls, striding over. "Bar was shot up. Scorpions."

"No," Liv cuts in, her voice sharp. "It wasn't them."

I freeze. "You saw who did it?"

She hesitates then glances down. That silence presses in like a vice.

"I saw Dagger," she says finally, voice quiet. "He found us in the bathroom. Told us to stay put 'til the cops showed."

I blink. "*Sorry, what?*"

She shrugs, but it's stiff. "He . . . he found us in the bathroom."

I pinch the bridge of my nose, trying to slow my thoughts before they spiral into violence. "You *spoke* to him?" Bria snorts a half-giggle. I turn my gaze on her, slow and cold, and the amusement dies on her lips. "Don't hold back," I say, my voice like ice.

"It's nothing," Liv snaps, throwing her sister a warning glare.

"If you don't tell me the truth, *he* will," I bite out. "And he'll do it with that smug fucking grin, and that will piss me off more and I'll do something stupid, something to stop him grinning ever again. So, Liv, what did he say that's got your sister acting like a giddy teenager?"

She hesitates. "He just called me beautiful." My stomach twists. Rage flares like a flame to fuel.

Bria jumps in, her tone singsong. "*He touched her cheek* and called her beautiful," she says, smiling wide. "And then he called her *his good girl.*"

My vision tunnels, blood roaring in my ears. Dagger had his hands on her. And he *fucking smiled* while he did it. I clench my fists so tight, my knuckles crack. My jaw's wired shut, teeth grinding like a slow-burn fuse.

Dagger touched her.

He called her beautiful.

He fucking called her *his good girl*.

"I'll kill him," I whisper. Not a threat, a promise. My voice is calm in the way a loaded gun is calm.

"Bully," Liv says quickly, stepping closer. Her hands come to my chest, grounding me. "He didn't hurt us. He could've, but he didn't. He kept the others out. He made sure we were safe."

"Oh, so now he's a *hero*?" I snarl. "That piece of shit walks in, touches you, plays protector, and you think that means something?"

Her face hardens. "I'm not *saying* that. I'm saying he had the chance to do damage and he *didn't*."

"Yet." My voice is razor-sharp. "But he *will*. That's what this is—a move. A warning. A fucking *game*."

Behind me, I hear Boss muttering into his phone, pulling strings and calling in favours. Smiler and Taz flank us like guards, eyes scanning for threats.

Liv lowers her voice, trying to steady mine. "He looked me in the eye, Bully. He knew exactly who I was, who I belonged to. And he still walked away. Why?"

"Because he wanted you to *tell* me." I meet her eyes, cold and steady. "This? All of this? It wasn't a favour. It was a fucking *message*. He touched what's mine, and now, I've got a decision to make." She flinches at the word 'mine' but doesn't argue.

"I didn't agree to you using me as a pawn in your macho game," she says.

I reach up and tuck a strand of her hair behind her ear, gentler than I feel. "You didn't, but you left the board, Liv. That's how he got close."

She looks away, guilt shadowing her face.

I step back, glancing over to where the guys are. "Boss, get me everything on Dagger's movements tonight. Who he came with. Who saw him leave."

"Already on it," Boss says grimly. "And Pres . . . we got a war coming."

I nod once, eyes still on Liv.

"No," she whispers. "You've had *a warning*. Don't turn it into a war." *Too late,* I think, but I don't say it.

I call church the second we get back, leaving Liv strict instructions to stay in the clubhouse. After tonight, I think she'll be following my orders.

The table is packed. Everyone who matters is here, patched members only. Doors locked. Voices low. Tension high.

I stand at the head of the table, arms crossed and jaw set. The overhead light casts deep shadows around the room, revealing brooding men ready for the fight, with fists clenched and eyes burning bright.

Boss finishes laying out a map of the area, red X's marking known Scorpion activity at bars, safe houses, and tonight's location.

"They knew," I say, voice low and steady. "They knew Liv was in that bar." No one speaks. The weight of those words drops like a gavel. "They didn't go in guns blazing to start a war. They went in to *prove a point*."

Taz leans forward, elbows on the table. "A warning."

Smiler nods. "They wanted her scared. Wanted *you* rattled."

"They got close *again*," I growl. "That's the part that matters."

Silence again, until Boss speaks. "Dagger sent a message. He walked into that bar, got close to your old lady, touched her face, called her *his good girl*," he says it with disgust, "and walked away before we even knew he was there. That's not a warning. That's a fucking *taunt*."

"Liv said he told them to stay hidden until the cops came," says Taz. "He knew we'd show. He wanted her to survive to deliver the story."

"And she did," I mutter bitterly. "Right to my face." I exhale hard and begin to pace. The fire inside me is raging again, and I'm barely holding it together. "This isn't about territory," I say. "It's not about deals or club business. This was *personal*. He wanted me to feel powerless. He wanted to see how far he could reach before I bled."

"And?" asks Smiler.

"I'm bleeding."

The room stiffens.

"So, what's the play?" Boss asks, voice tight.

I stop pacing and look around the table. Everyone's eyes are on me, waiting. "We don't retaliate tonight." I'm met with murmurs, a few raised brows, but no one interrupts. "We don't play checkers when Dagger's playing chess. He wants fire, we give him *fear*. We pull his resources apart, piece by piece. We find his weak link, and then we *bury* it."

"And Liv?" Taz asks carefully.

"She doesn't leave the clubhouse without two men. Eyes on her at all times until this is over." I clench my fists until my knuckles turn white. "I want everything we know about Dagger, every side deal, every burner number, every favour he's called in the last few months. I want to know who let him into that bar, and I want to know why I didn't see it coming." I slam my fist on the table. "We hit back, but we do it *my way*."

Chairs scrape back as I slam the gavel down. Brothers file out, already texting contacts, calling in watchers. Moving like the hive just got poked.

I stare at the map, my brow furrowed. It's personal. *Why?* I don't even know Dagger. And, yeah, the clubs have bad history that dates back since forever, but something about this feels different.

Smiler lingers. "You good, brother?"

"No," I mutter, "but I will be. Once Dagger learns what it feels like to fear *me*."

CHAPTER TEN

Olivia

I'm sitting in the window seat of the bedroom with my knees tucked to my chest, waiting for Bully to get out of church.

I fucked up, I know I did, but surely it was just a coincidence Dagger was there. Maybe it was him who was under attack? Because if it was the Scorpions like Boss said, then why didn't he take me? Or at least hurt me? I shudder, remembering the way his eyes pierced mine, and then I find myself smiling. Bria's right, it was hot.

The door opens and Bully enters, his head lowered. It shuts behind him with a heavy click, like it's feeding off his mood. I watch as he shrugs from his kutte and throws it over the chair. The silence between us is thick and heavy, like everything we just said outside that bar is waiting here, hanging between us.

"You're mad," I say, dropping my feet to the floor and curling my fingers over the edge of the window seat.

"I'm trying not to be," he mutters, still avoiding looking at me.

I scoff. "Could've fooled me."

He runs a hand through his hair. It's already messed, like he's done it a thousand times. A sure sign he's stressed. "I thought you were dead, Liv."

"I didn't think—"

"No," he snaps, cutting me off. "You didn't. You turned your phone off. You left the club, knowing damn well the Scorpions have been circling. And for what? A drink with 'your girls'."

I resent the way he says 'girls', like I'm a child, and I bristle at his words. "If he wanted to hurt me, he's had plenty of chances."

He arches a brow, flexing his fingers like he's fighting not to grab me and shake some sense into me. "Are you trying to fucking piss me off?" he asks, his tone dangerously low. "What does that even mean, Liv? Is there shit I should know?"

I groan. "No, of course not. Look, I don't want to be locked away here. I want my normal life, the one I had before you got out."

"There is no normal anymore," he yells, slamming his palm against the wall. "Not when you're the old lady to the President. You're a target, Liv, whether you like it or not."

I flinch. "What are you saying, Bully? That I can never go out? Never see my friends?"

He takes a deep breath. "I'm just trying to keep you alive."

I blink back the tears that balance dangerously on my lower lashes. "I was scared tonight. When that shot first rang out, I couldn't breathe. I kept it together for Bria. I didn't fall apart." He remains quiet, and I risk a step closer. "But I need you to stop treating me like I already have. Like I can't handle being at your side."

He takes my hands gently. "You were brave. But darlin' . . . *he touched you*. He looked you in the eye and said those things because he wanted *me* to hear them in your voice."

We stand in silence for a beat. "I'm sorry," I say.

He pulls me against his chest, resting his chin on my head. "Just don't make me go through that again. I can't protect you if I don't know where you are."

"Things are moving so fast . . ." I begin.

He pulls back to look me in the eye. "Don't start with the doubts again, Liv. I can't take anymore."

I see a flicker of vulnerability as his fingers dig into my arm, like he's trying to convey how much I mean to him, how much he needs me. "So much has changed," I mutter, looking around the room. "You're on the top floor," I add with a slight smile. When I first started dating Bully, he had a room between Boss and Taz, a tag team of self-professed whores. Their constant one-night stands kept me awake with cries of ecstasy or headboards banging either side of us. It was hell. And now, we're on the top floor in what's basically a self-contained apartment.

"My parents were the last people to stay in here," he mutters, glancing around. "Hawk had it redecorated after Dad died, but he hated it up here, felt too far away from the others." He laughs, shaking his head. "I can't say I blame him. It does feel weird being up here and away from the noise of the club."

"I like it," I say. "And the music from the bar won't keep me awake."

He grins, wrapping his arms around my waist. "It'll be perfect for when we have babies."

I frown. We used to talk about marriage and kids, but once he got sent away, I put it to the back of my mind. "One day," I say with a shrug.

"Soon," he adds, running his fingers into my hair and tipping my head back. "Real soon." He kisses me, stealing my breath.

"I'm on birth control," I tell him, and he frowns. It's not something he's asked about, so I never thought to mention it until now, but the way his eyes are burning again, I can see it's going to be an issue. I pull back to sit on the edge of the bed to remove my shoes.

"Why?"

"Because . . ."

"Liv, I've been inside for five years. Why the fuck are you on birth control?"

I roll my eyes, dropping my shoes on the floor and standing. "It doesn't have to be a big deal, Bully."

"So, why do I feel like it is?"

"I was having heavy periods. The doctor suggested the coil to help. Jesus, you have to make an issue out of everything," I mutter, beginning to undress.

He watches, his eyes softening. "Well, when can you have it out?"

"I don't want it out."

"You do," he says, sidling up to me with a smile. "I wanna fill you with babies."

I roll my eyes, batting his hands away as he removes my bra. "So you can keep me here in your tower of bikers? No chance."

He runs kisses over my collarbone. "No, so I can have lots of little Livs wrapping me round their fingers." He groans against my neck. "Just thinking about you round with my baby makes me hard."

"One day," I say firmly. "But you have a war to fight, remember?"

Bully

The next day, church reeks of smoke and bloodlust. I stand at the head of the table, arms braced against the scarred wood. My kutte creaks under the strain of my tense shoulders. "All right," I say. "Let's get everything we've got. Lay it out."

Boss clicks the laptop, and the projector hums to life, casting a grainy image of Dagger's face on the wall. Even in a still photo, he looks smug.

"Dagger. President of the Scorpions. Before that, an enforcer. Smart operator. Doesn't drink on runs, doesn't screw around in public, doesn't get caught," Boss says.

"Military?" I ask.

"Not officially, but he moves like it."

Whizz speaks up from the corner. "His enforcer is ex-Forces for sure. Viper. Honourable discharge, then went ghost for a while. Shows up again in a weapons ring out of Manchester."

"Tech?" I ask.

"Patch," says Brains, flipping through his notes. "Quiet, weird. Good with burners. We know he reroutes calls through six countries before they hit a SIM card. Same guy handles their accounts, too."

"They got an auto shop just outside of Notts in Mansfield," adds Stretch. "And a strip joint there too. Laundering front, cash-heavy. I've got eyes on both."

Ragnar leans forward, tattoos catching the light. "Their street crew's getting louder. Word is they've taken over two corners from local dealers. If they're not careful, they'll have more wars. I've already had two big timers call me for backup, Pres. We made the deal with them to run the drugs as long as they were cutting clean. Now, they're calling for our protection."

Tally sneers. "They're not expanding cos they're smart. They're expanding cos they think they can *take us*."

Smiler lights a smoke and exhales slow. "Yeah, but none of that explains why Dagger walked into that bar *himself*. Presidents don't do grunt work. Not unless it's personal."

The room falls silent. That's what's been chewing at me since Liv told me. He didn't send a soldier. He went in alone. Found *her*. Touched her face. Whispered that she was a 'good girl' like he'd known her his whole damn life.

And he let her walk out.

"Maybe he's fixated on Liv," says Lords. "Wants to rattle you."

"That's a death wish," mutters Taz.

But Boss frowns. "Nah. This wasn't a stalker play. He wasn't trying to *keep* her. He was trying to send a message. Not just to you, to *all* of us."

I slam my palm against the table. "Then what the fuck's he trying to say?"

No one answers. There's just the hum of the projector and the quiet hiss of Smiler's cigarette. "Could be grief," says Brains quietly. "We've seen it before. A death that twists someone up, turns it into a vendetta. Could be we missed something. Something old."

"Like what?"

He shrugs. "No names in the system. But if he lost someone and thinks *we* had a hand in it . . ."

I straighten and my jaw tenses. "I'd know," I snap. But deep down, I'm not so sure. "Keep digging," I bark. "Check old prison records. Smiler, you said he had an ex, find out about her. Or any woman tied to him, even family, whatever. Find out who she was and if she crossed our path."

"You thinking what I'm thinking?" Taz mutters under his breath.

"That he didn't go there for Liv. He went there *because of me*."

"Exactly."

"I don't even know what I did." I check my watch. "We meet out front at one. a.m. No excuses. Ready to roll out."

—◄⊖✦⊖►—

The bass thumps through the pavement like a heartbeat trying too hard. Outside, the neon sign flickers "Venom" in cracked red light.

I nod once, and the van rolls to the curb, no headlights.

"Taz, Smiler, Ragnar, Stretch, and Lords, you're in with me," I instruct. "Boss and Whizz, run distraction at the back."

The power grid is ready to go, and a jammer blocking the place from pinging for help has been set up. No one's getting out until we're done.

"Keep it clean," I mutter, strapping on my gloves. "No bodies. This is a message, not a war cry."

Smiler smirks. "What's the message?"

I look up at the building, jaw tight. "You got close. Now, we're closer."

Taz kicks the service door in. The bouncer barely gets a blink before Ragnar drops him with a taser and drags him out the way. Inside, it's red lights and a stale stench of sex. Whizz kills the power, and the music stops. The perfect sound of chaos fills the air—girls screaming, clients panicking, mixed with our heavy boots.

Stretch heads to the DJ booth and starts the playlist we brought. "Can't Stop" by Red Hot Chili Peppers blasts out, bringing a smile to my face.

I walk straight to the office. Dagger's not here—we knew he wouldn't be—but we're not here for *him*. The office reeks of stale cigars and leather polish. His chair spins slowly, abandoned.

I plant the crowbar into the desk drawers while Taz checks the safe. There's nothing but cash and a loaded Glock, all untouched.

"Don't take the money," I say. "Leave it. Let them wonder why we *didn't*."

I grab a photo off the wall, a framed picture of Dagger and his crew raising drinks around this very room. I slam it to the floor, shattering glass across the carpet.

"Tag it," I order.

Smiler steps up, pulls a can of spray paint from his jacket, and scrawls across the wall in thick black letters:

YOU MISSED. WE WON'T.

Stretch pours petrol over the broken glass and office floor, just enough to burn but not enough to kill. We're halfway down the stairs when Boss radios in.

"Security feeds are scrubbed. Time to roll."

I take one last look over the club, red lights blinking, girls huddled near the exit, bouncers on their knees with their hands behind their heads. *Good*. They'll remember the fear.

I flick the lighter and toss it over the railing. It lands with a *whumpf*, fire crawling fast across the floor like it's hungry.

We're out and gone in sixty seconds. Our van pulls away without a trace, just as the first plume of smoke rises into the sky.

In the rearview mirror, Taz grins. "Think he'll get the message this time?"

I stare ahead, fists clenched. "No, but maybe he'll be tempted to fill us in on why he's coming for us . . . or *me*."

The club is quiet when we return. Not the peaceful kind, the waiting kind. Like the walls know we've done something tonight, and now, they're holding their breath for the fallout. Because there *will* be more retaliation, more nights like this one.

I head upstairs to my floor and toe off my boots at the door. I creep into the bedroom and shrug off my kutte, careful not to wake Liv. The scent of smoke clings to me, bitter and sharp, but all I want to do is feel her against me. The moonlight spills across the bed, catching on Liv's bare shoulder where the blankets have slipped down. She's curled up on my side, peaceful, blissfully unaware of the storm surrounding her.

I strip off silently and slip beneath the sheets. She stirs as I slide behind her, wrapping my arm around her waist and pulling her into me. I hum in pleasure as her soft, warm body presses against my own.

"Bully?" she whispers, her voice heavy with sleep.

"Yeah, baby," I murmur against her hair.

"Where were you?"

I press a kiss to the back of her neck, fingers brushing her stomach. "Handling shit."

She doesn't ask more. She knows better. But I feel her body tense, just for a second, like she *knows* exactly who it involved. I hold her tighter.

She turns in my arms, her hand sliding up to rest against my chest. Her fingers find the rhythm of my heart. "You smell like fire," she murmurs. "You didn't retaliate, did you?"

I close my eyes. "Sleep," I whisper.

"You can change this place, Bully. It's your chance to make it different. Safe."

I don't answer. Deep down, part of the addiction to this life is the danger. But sitting back and letting Dagger touch my old lady, breathe the same air as her, is like inviting him in to take everything that's mine. Personal or not, if I sit back and stay quiet, he'll just keep coming until the only thing my club has left is the tattoo on our backs.

CHAPTER ELEVEN

Olivia

The smell of coffee and bacon grease hits me before I even reach the kitchen. Bria trails behind, yawning.

The kitchen's already crowded. A couple club girls are perched on countertops, giggling over something on a phone. Poodle's flipping pancakes like she's mad at them. I spot *her* immediately. *Poison*. Her bleach-blonde hair falling in perfect waves around her shoulders, her lips dripping in gloss. She's sitting away from the rest, tapping away on her mobile with a slight smirk on her face.

Bria gives me a shove forward, reminding me why I woke her to come down here with me. It's not that I'm scared of the club whores, but I need to show them I'm in charge around here now. It's club rules one-o-one.

As I step into the kitchen farther, she glances up, her smile fading. She's probably trying to work out what my game is, because it's pretty clear she thinks she's in charge around here. "Morning, ladies," I say, keeping my tone bright. "Sleep well?" I ask as I grab the coffee pot.

"Define sleep," mutters Poodle, taking the pancake stack to the table, the plate thudding as she slams it down. "And this is my third day in a row of doing breakfast," she adds, her tone exasperated.

"Quit whining," snaps Poison.

"Who's turn was it today?" I ask, filling Bria's cup too.

Poodle glances in Poison's direction but doesn't answer. Her look tells me enough. "Maybe you need a rota," I suggest. The scoff from where Poison remains seated gets my attention. "You don't agree?"

"We work things out between ourselves," she spits. "Besides, don't you have enough to worry about with your man setting the city ablaze for you?" I narrow my eyes, and she smiles wide, realising I have no idea what she's talking about. "I guess he didn't tell you about his little midnight trip over to Mansfield?"

"It's not our business what the men do," I say through gritted teeth, pissed that she clearly knows something I don't.

She shrugs. "I just think your time would be better taking care of our President than interfering in what we get up to."

"I'm the President's old lady," I say firmly. "That means I've got a role here, keeping things in check. Starting with the club whores."

She arches a brow, the smirk already spreading. "Oh? So, now, you think you're in charge?" She laughs. "We don't need a pimp."

"Enough," snaps Bria. "Show some fucking respect, unless you want this getting back to Bully."

The smirk twists cruel. She pushes to her feet slowly, like she's got all day to play this game. "You think the Pres has time for bitchy squabbles?" she asks. "Last night, the Scorpions' strip joint went up like a matchbox, all in the name of his old lady."

"Shut your mouth," Bria hisses. We all know the bikers would lose their shit if they heard us talking club business.

"Imagine causing all this heat," she says lightly, eyes gleaming as they lock on me. "How long will it be before you get him killed?"

"This wasn't because of me," I snap, my heart pounding.

She tilts her head. "Oh, baby, open your eyes. He torched that place *for you.* He dragged the club into war, all because you needed his attention."

"What?" My blood runs cold.

"We all know that's why you started talking to Dagger. Pres wasn't falling at your feet when he got out, so you just had to get his attention. What better way than to pick a guy he can't back down from?"

My mouth opens, but nothing comes out. For a split second, the room feels too small, like the air's been sucked out of it and left behind a vacuum full of judgment.

Bria's already in motion, stepping between us. "Say one more thing," she warns, her voice sharp enough to cut, "and I swear to god, you'll be picking your teeth off the floor."

I barely hear her. My mind races with protest, hating that the entire club might think I've been playing some kind of game. *I haven't.* I didn't even know who Dagger was when Bria dragged him over to cheer me up. And that's all I wanted, a distraction. A reason to forget Bully. I never wanted any of this, least of all a war.

"So, like I said, take care of the Pres, cos who knows what could happen if he gets distracted."

My head snaps up to meet her eyes. "What's that supposed to mean?"

"Yeah, Poison, what does that mean?" asks Birdy. "It sounded like a threat."

"I'm just saying, we all know what Bully is like, right? If she doesn't take care of his needs when he's so stressed, he might get . . . distracted." She smirks. "And I, for one, am happy to step in and help when he requests it." She saunters past me, knocking her shoulder into mine as she passes.

"Bully needs to know about this," says Bria firmly.

"No," I snap before she can stomp off. "I'll deal with it." I look the rest of the women in the eye before adding, "I didn't do any of this on purpose." They remain silent. "Poodle, draw up a fair rota. One that means Poison pulls her weight, because if she doesn't start to, she's out." And I turn on my heel and leave.

I break out into the sunshine and inhale until my lungs stretch painfully full then release it slow. My pulse begins to settle, but the unease lingers. It's too quiet out here.

The clubhouse sits deep in an industrial compound, the kind of place only lorries find, parking up to sleep off long-haul hours. Normally, the silence brings peace. Today, it feels like a warning.

I slip around the back of the building, out of sight from the road. The weight in my chest still hasn't lifted. I sink down beneath a tree, knees pulled close, and try to untangle the mess inside my head.

My phone buzzes in my pocket. *Darren.* Shit. I forgot he had my number. I hesitate before unlocking it.

> **Darren: Don't freak out. I just wanted to check you're okay.**

I stare at the message, heart thudding again. It doesn't read like a threat, but I know I should show Bully. Before I can stand, another one comes through.

> **Darren: This was never about you, Olivia. I'm sorry you're caught up in it.**

My thumb hovers over the reply. I shouldn't answer. I *know* I shouldn't.

But after what Poison said . . . maybe I need to hear it from someone else. Someone who might actually tell me the truth.

> **Me: Did you know who I was right from the beginning?**

His reply is instant.

> **Darren: Yes.**

The air catches in my throat. I'd expected him to lie. Or maybe I'd *hoped* this was some awful accident, that I was just a coincidence.

> **Me: So this whole time, you were using me to get to him?**

> **Darren: No.**

> **Me: Then what was the plan? Because right now, I feel like I've fucked up everything.**

> **Darren: You were never the target, Olivia. Know that. And I won't let anything bad happen to you.**

> **Me: Who is the target?**

A pause.

> **Darren: I think we both know the answer to that. Someone like you shouldn't be in this life. If he cared about you, he'd let you go.**

I stare at the screen, my pulse thudding like a war drum.

> **Me: Hurting him will hurt me.**

> **Darren: I know. That's the part that makes this hard. But sometimes people need to be hurt to see the truth. You're protecting a man who doesn't deserve it. He leaves a trail of wreckage behind him, Olivia. You just haven't seen it all yet. You will. And when you do, I hope you remember I tried to warn you.**

Bully

The sun's out, but it doesn't touch the chill riding up my spine. Liv bolted out the clubhouse like her skin didn't fit right, and I gave her space because Bria asked me to. I left her to breathe, but five minutes turned to ten, and my gut began twisting like something was wrong.

I find her behind the building, tucked under the shade of a tree like she's trying to disappear. Her shoulders are hunched, phone in hand, and I'm close enough to see her thumbs fly across the screen. I breathe a sigh of relief and take a step closer. She doesn't hear me, and I move until I'm behind the tree.

The name at the top of her screen catches my eye. ***Darren.*** I freeze, my blood roaring.

Her head dips, reading. She doesn't even sense me behind her. That's how deep in it she is. My jaw tightens as she types again, and another message flashes up before she can close the screen.

I hope you remember I tried to warn you.

That's all I need to see. I reach forward and *snatch* the phone out her hands. She gasps and spins, wide-eyed.

"Bully—"

I don't hear her. All I see is red. My hands are shaking, but I keep my voice low, deadly calm.

"How long has he been messaging you?"

She stares at me, frozen. Then, she softly says, "He was just checking in."

"Checking in?" I repeat, as my own heartbeat pounds in my ears. I tilt the phone towards her. "This doesn't look like checking in. This looks like a fuckin' connection."

"I was trying to find out what his problem is."

I scan the messages, each one lighting another piece of rage inside me. "Jesus, Liv. You're literally conversing with the fucking enemy," I yell, unable to hide my anger.

"I was about to come and show you," she mutters, barely a whisper.

"When?" I hiss, stepping forward so she's forced to move back until her spine hits the tree. "After he laid out his next hit? After he twisted your head so far round, you didn't know who the fuck you're loyal to anymore?"

Her eyes flash with hurt. "I'm loyal to you."

I exhale hard through my nose. My hands are still shaking. Rage and fear are bleeding together, making it hard to think straight.

I lower the phone, stepping in closer until my mouth is to her ear. "In case I haven't been clear, you're not to talk to him again. Delete his fucking number. Block him. Because next time, Liv . . . next time I find out you're in contact with the man who wants me dead . . ." I let the sentence hang heavy with everything I'm not saying.

She swallows hard. Her chin lifts like I've slapped her. I realise I'm standing over her like a storm, casing her in and keeping her close enough to feel the anger vibrating from me. She's looking at me like I'm a stranger, like she doesn't know who the fuck I am.

Her phone's still hot in my hand. I want to crush it, throw it, grind it into the gravel until the screen doesn't scream *Darren* at me anymore.

Instead, I breathe hard through my nose and wait for her to speak.

"I didn't reply to hurt you," she says, her voice tight. "I just . . . I needed answers. After what Poison said—"

I grit my teeth so hard, my jaw pops. "Poison doesn't know shit. Don't go listening to clubhouse drama like it's gospel."

Liv's shoulders stiffen. "She said I started a war." Her eyes meet mine, and this time, they don't flinch. "That the fire last night at the Scorpions' strip club was because of me." I hold her stare, not able to lie but bound by club rules to keep our shit quiet. "Jesus, Bully," she cries, shoving me back a step and putting space between us.

"It was a message," I say, my voice steady and measured.

"A message?" Her mouth falls open. "You torched a building because of me. Someone could've gotten hurt."

"I did it because of them. Because they walked into that bar, knowing you were there, and shot it up. That wasn't random, Liv. That was bait."

"That you could have ignored. Where will it end?"

"With bloodshed, maybe death," I mutter.

"So, stop it now before it goes that far."

My eyes reach hers. "You know I can't."

A sob escapes her, and she rushes to me, grabbing my arms desperately. "Yes, you can. They'll come back at you for last night, but you don't have to do anything else. I won't message him. I won't ever speak to him again. Just walk away."

I want to laugh, to tell her how stupid and naïve she's being. "Do you think I wanted this, Liv?" I ask. There's so much fear, I can hardly catch a breath. "That I wanted you to be caught up in this? That I want you anywhere near it?"

"You get to decide—"

I slam my hand against the tree, and she cries out in surprise, flinching. "If I don't fight back, Liv, shall I tell you what will happen?" I yell. "They'll kill us. Me, Taz, Boss . . . they'll wipe us out like we're nothing and they'll take everything. Every shipment, every weapon from here to Russia, will be in their hands. An entire lifetime's work for this club gone because you couldn't follow my fucking rules." She gasps, not bothering to swipe her tears away as they trickle down her cheeks. "So, don't ask me to sit by while they taunt me by using my own. Fucking. Wife."

I drop her mobile to the ground and crush it under my boot, the satisfaction easing my anger. "This life will *always* come with blood," I warn, pinching her chin in my fingers and forcing her to look me in the eye. "I didn't start this, Liv, but I'll burn every fucking piece of them down if it keeps you safe."

The clubhouse is thick with smoke and tension. The door shuts behind me, muffling the outside world as my brothers gather for church. Misty jumps down from my chair, a spot she seems to frequent like she's keeping it warm for me.

"Alright, talk to me," I say, cutting through the weight in the air.

"There's still a heavy presence," says Boss. "If anything, they've increased their movements."

"The fact they're not hiding doesn't mean they ain't scared," says Taz, tapping his lighter on the table.

"He reached out to Liv," I mutter, and all eyes fix on me. "Texted her," I add. "I should've took her mobile, but I didn't think, and that's on me."

"When?" asks Taz, his expression full of anger.

"Half-hour ago."

"What did he say?" asks Boss.

"Checking in with her." I give a cold, empty laugh and push to stand in irritation. I pace behind my chair. "Imagine that, he's checking in on *my* old lady, like it's his fucking job." I shake my head.

"He's taking the piss," mutters Taz.

"Did anything come back on his associates?" I ask.

We all look over to Whizz, who's hunched over his laptop, his eyes bloodshot and his fingers twitching over the keys like he's trying to crack the devil's own vault. He doesn't look up, just tilts the screen towards me. "Yeah, you're gonna want to sit back down for this."

He clicks open a series of folders. Screenshots. Spreadsheets. Names. Numbers.

"Shit, Whizz, have you been at this all night?" asks Taz.

"You wanted answers, I've got them," he mutters, his brow furrowed as he opens the folder he wants us to see. "I started by checking payments. There're loads connected to the Scorpions' affiliated businesses, but I focussed on the UK ones first. There's a fake security company just out of Manchester. It doesn't run guards, it runs money." He pulls up a map and pins stretch across it like bullet holes. "They're laundering through their strip clubs, which we pretty much suspected, but they also have betting shops and a fake construction company. But the money trail gets interesting here," he taps the screen, "when it jumps offshore."

"Where to?" Boss asks, leaning closer to see the screen.

"Malta, Belize, and back to London. The loop is tight. Clean. Would've missed it if I hadn't cross-referenced transaction times."

I nod once. "So, what are they hiding?"

"Guns, for sure. Maybe drugs. But after looking at this empire, I reckon they're just using that to throw us off. Make us think they're no real threat to our business. But in the background, they're shifting weapons, ready to make a move when they bring us down." He takes a deep breath, releasing it slowly as he clicks open another folder. "Here's the kicker. See this shell company?" He zooms in on one labelled 'Griffin Holdings Ltd.' "It's been wiring payments to a third-party logistics company . . . that also did work with a buyer we sold bikes to last year."

I freeze. "Are you saying they're trying to pin us for their shit?"

"I'm saying there's a trail that looks like we've done business with them. Whether it's staged or not, I don't know yet, but it puts us in the firing line if the heat turns up."

I lean over the desk, eyes narrowing. "Anyone in our crew tied to those payments?"

"Still working on that, Pres. They've a shit tonne to go through."

"You need extra eyes?"

He nods, and Tally raises a hand to offer. I give him the nod.

"Keep digging. Discreetly. And if you find out anyone's feeding them info, I want to know before they draw another breath."

He nods and turns back to the screen. "Already on it, Pres."

CHAPTER TWELVE

Olivia

The men have been holed up in church for hours, and without my mobile phone to occupy me, I've turned my attention to the rota Birdy and Poodle have worked on. They're watching me with bated breath as I look it over, and when I nod in approval, they relax. "It's missing a couple people, though," I say, and Poodle frowns, taking it back and scanning it.

"I literally have everyone," she says, her brow furrowed.

"Me and Bria."

She looks up. "You're the Pres's old lady," she says with an amused expression like my words are absurd.

"We all have to pull our weight," I say, taking the rota back and adding my name down for two nights of cooking. "Bria is a terrible cook, but she won't mind cleanup," I say, adding her in for dishes and bin duties. "I'll also help with other things when I'm not at work." They exchange a confused look. "What?" I ask.

"You work?"

I laugh. "Yeah. Well, when the club isn't locked down, that is. Good job I have an understanding boss."

"And Bully doesn't mind?" asks Birdy.

I slide into a seat beside Poodle. "Maybe. He hasn't mentioned it. But I'm not relying on the club to support me if things go wrong."

"What would go wrong?" asks Poodle.

I shrug. "If Bully and I don't work out."

"But he claimed you," says Birdy, giving an unsure laugh. "Don't you have to make it work?"

"We've had our issues," I say. "Most of which involve this club. And while I know this life is . . . different, I refuse to put my heart and soul into it and let my old life go."

Poodle gives a sympathetic smile. "You're worried he'll end up in prison again?"

I look away, scared she's seeing far more than I mean her to. "Anyway, get this rota up, and if anyone is slacking, let me know and I'll sort it."

Birdy smiles. "You're alright," she says, and I return her smile.

"Not as bad as some are saying, right?"

The door opens and Bully fills it. Just by the look on his face, I can see he's still moody. The other two leave without a word, probably sensing the dark cloud that hangs over him. I follow him with my eyes as he goes to the coffee pot and fills a mug, then he turns to leave. I roll my eyes in irritation just as Bria enters, passing him and joining me at the table.

"You okay?" she asks.

I shrug. "He's ignoring me."

"Enjoy the peace," she says with a grin. "What happened?"

"Darren, or Dagger, texted me. Somehow, that's my fault."

She gives a giggle. "Oooh, conversing with the enemy."

I smirk. "It's not funny."

"What's Bully so worried about? You're locked-up here. It's not like you can run away with the other big, bad biker."

"It's the disrespect he's pissed about."

She scoffs. "*Rude*. Is he saying Dagger doesn't like you and he's just using you to get to him?" I nod. "Or maybe he just thought you were fit."

I laugh, pushing to stand. "Whatever you do, don't say that to Bully. He'll blow a gasket."

I find him in his office, talking to Poison. She gives me a smug smile the second she sees me, and just like that, my hackles rise.

Bully looks stressed. And tired. There's a line between his brows that wasn't there yesterday, and guilt punches me in the gut. I'm part of what's weighing him down.

"I'm happy for you to sort it," he tells Poison, then looks at me. "Poison said you okayed a rota." I narrow my eyes, already feeling heat rise in my chest. "It's not going to work," he adds.

"Thanks, Pres," Poison purrs, smiling like she's just won something before swaying out the door.

I step into the room, closing the distance. "Why not? Why overrule it without talking to me?"

He exhales, long and tired, like the world's on his back and I've just added another stone. "Because I don't care, Liv. I don't have time for drama over who's wiping the damn table or emptying the bin."

"All the girls were fine with it except her. Poison's just a lazy cow." Misty taps my foot with her paw, and I crouch down to give her a quick stroke.

He arches a brow. "Name-calling? Seriously?"

"I was trying to help," I snap. "Trying to take some of the pressure off you."

He rubs his brow, jaw clenched like he's holding back a full eruption. "Just leave the club shit to me, yeah?"

I stand, and Misty totters off to Bully, lying by his chair. His words sting more than they should. "Then what exactly *is* my role, Bully?" I challenge.

He looks at me, guarded and worn out. "To look after me, Liv." His voice drops. "If you can manage that in between flirting with Dagger."

I feel like he's given me a blow to the chest, and I stagger back a step. "*Fuck you,* Bully."

I turn to leave, but his voice stops me cold. "Whizz is digging, Liv. If there's anything you need to tell me, now's the time."

I spin around slowly, my pulse thudding in my ears. "Like what?" His eyes meet mine, pleading, searching. He doesn't say it outright, but I know what he's asking. "You think *I'm* feeding the Scorpions?" My voice is a low growl, sharp with betrayal.

He doesn't blink. "Are you?" I stare at him, stunned. "Are you?" he repeats.

My jaw tightens, breath catching like something sharp in my throat. "Wow." My voice is soft, bitter. "After everything, *that's* what you think of me?" He doesn't answer, doesn't deny it. Just watches me with those tired, guarded eyes like he's waiting for me to prove him right. My heart cracks a little then crumbles completely. "You don't trust me," I whisper.

He looks away. That's all the answer I need.

"Five years, Bully. Five long fucking years I've waited. And you know . . ." I hiss, stepping closer and pointing my finger at him. "You *know* I haven't cheated because you had someone watching me." I scoff, shaking my head in anger. "You asked me to stay, made me think this could all be worth it, and the second shit gets hard, you turn on me like I'm some random bitch off the street." I step closer, my fury burning over. "I have told you everything that happened with Dagger. *Everything.* You saw us on the CCTV, so you know I never left with him, kissed him, or even flirted. I have *never* crossed the line. I have *never* cheated on you. Never given reason for you to think otherwise, and still, you think I'd sell you out?"

His jaw ticks, but he stays silent. "I was trying to help by putting the rota in because the girls are sick of Poison slacking. I didn't want them to turn to you because you're already under so much pressure. And the second my back is turned, she comes crying to you and you overrule me. How the hell are they ever gonna take me seriously if you can't? And how will anyone in this club trust me if my own old man doesn't?"

I take a steadying breath. "Yah know what it tells women like Poison when you do shit like that? That we're not a team. That you don't support me. It shows her the cracks she's waiting for to claw her way between us." I head for the door. "I'm done begging for a seat at your table, Bully. I don't fit here."

I storm out before the emotion spills its way out of me completely. If I stay, I'll break, and I'm tired of breaking for someone who doesn't see me.

Bully

The door slams, and the silence that follows is louder than her shouting.

I sit back in my chair, heart pounding like I just went a round in the cage. Only this feels worse. There's no blood to mop up, no crowd to drown it out. Just me and the echo of her voice still ringing in my ears. *"You don't trust me."*

She's right.

And, fuck, I hate that because it means *he's* winning. Dagger is coming between us, causing doubt. Doing what he set out to do.

I rub my hands over my face, dragging them down like it'll take the weight with them. It doesn't. I feel heavier, like I'm carrying guilt I can't name and regret I'm too damn proud to admit. I replay her words, every one of them sharper than the last. *"We're not a team . . . I'm done begging for a place at your table . . ."*

Goddamn it.

I wanted to protect her, to keep her out of all this. But somewhere along the line, I stopped seeing her and started seeing a liability. Another threat I couldn't control. Liv's never been the weak spot—I am. Because she matters . . . too fucking much.

The worst part? I saw the hurt before she even spoke and I still let it happen. I still accused her.

I slam my fist on the desk. The sound echoes, but it's not enough. Nothing is.

Whizz is digging into the Scorpions, and the closer we get to the truth, the more twisted it all feels. Liv might've been the one caught in the crossfire, but I'm the one who lit the fuse. And if I lose her? That might be the one price I can't afford.

The office door opens, and Whizz stands there with a grim expression, laptop balanced in one hand and his mobile in the other.

"We got some information on Dagger's wife." I frown as he enters, placing the computer on my desk. "She's dead. Suspected suicide," he side-eyes me, "which fits with our grief theory. But I also traced a few payments around the time of her death, and it looks suspicious." He turns the laptop to me. "Her name was Lila Carson." The room stills, and my lungs stop working. *Lila*. Her picture stares back at me, filling the screen and mocking me. I can almost hear her laughter ring out.

"You alright, Pres?" he asks.

I force a nod. "Call church," I mutter. "I'll be right there." I need a moment to compose myself.

Ten minutes later, I head in to find everyone seated. Lila's image is on the big screen, and I avoid looking at it as I turn to Whizz. "Get it off screen," I mutter.

"But, Pres, I—"

"Get it down," I yell, slamming the gavel down as he rushes to click off the image. "Go over what you know so far," I add, bracing my hands on the edge of the table and lowering my head.

"Lila Carson. Wife of Darren Carson, or as we know him, Dagger. It's the anniversary of her death this month. Two years." He glances my way before adding. "She was a prison officer."

"Where?" asks Taz, looking back and forth between me and Whizz like he already knows the answer.

"Lincoln," we answer in unison.

"She was on my wing," I add, my tone lower.

"She was suspended," Whizz continues, "and supposedly took her own life six months later, right before her disciplinary hearing."

"Supposedly?" Boss queries.

"Yeah. I went over some transactions that stood out around that time." Whizz clicks some buttons, and the screen appears up on the board again. "That one is to the previous crime commissioner," he states, "or an offshore company he owns. I'm suspecting it's why the story never made the news."

"Of her death?" asks Taz.

"That, and the fact she was suspended from her job."

"Why would any of that make the news?" asks Lords.

I take a breath. "Because she was suspended for gross misconduct," I mutter, not meeting anyone's eyes. "Engaging in an inappropriate sexual relationship with a prisoner."

Silence falls over the room. I hold my breath, waiting for them to catch on.

Taz is the first to move, his hand slams down on the table, the sound sharp. "Jesus, Pres. You fucked a screw?"

I scrub a hand down my face and sink into the seat beside him. "It was more than that," I say, my voice rough with disgust. "For her, anyway."

"Wait . . . how the fuck did she get that job if she was married to a criminal?" Boss asks, frowning.

"I can answer that," Whizz says, already pulling something up on his screen. "They paid for her to get in."

He taps the screen, showing a digital trail of transaction exchanges. "Money from the Scorpions went to the crime commissioner. He's since retired but still sits on the board of governors at Lincoln. I think she was their inside mule, bringing in class A for the gangs to sell."

I nod once. "She smuggled in gear."

"And you didn't think this would come back on us?" Taz snaps.

"It was a fuck," I growl, heat rising in my chest. "She was easy. I was bored. Five years inside, fighting to breathe, sometimes you take what comes."

"You didn't know she was tied to the Scorpions?" Boss asks quietly.

I glare at him until he drops his gaze. "If I'd known, I sure as shit wouldn't have touched her. She said she was married. I didn't ask questions that didn't concern me."

"Well, they concern all of us now," Boss mutters. Guilt coils tight in my chest. All this . . . everything . . . is because of me. And I've been blaming Liv.

I groan, tipping my head back to stare at the ceiling.

"It's no coincidence they've turned the heat up this month," Lords says, "with it being the anniversary of her death."

"Wait," Whizz says, scrolling fast. "I told you I found more tied to her death. Payments to the commissioner were just the start. The governor and prison director also got big payouts, but get this . . . Dagger led it all."

We all freeze.

"He had her fired," Whizz continues. "Set her tribunal date six months after the dismissal. All of it timed down to the day. Another officer reported the relationship, but no formal file was made. It went to the governor, then the director . . . then to Dagger." He leans forward, eyes sharp. "He orchestrated the whole thing. He made her suffer. And I don't think she killed herself—I think he did it and covered it up as suicide. Made it look like her depression took her under." He shrugs. "But it's plausible. She was facing a criminal investigation after the tribunal. It's illegal for a person of authority in a custodial setting to engage in sexual activity with someone in their care, even if consensual. It actually comes under the Sexual Offences Act."

"Did you know she was dead?" asks Taz.

I give my head a slight shake, the weight of it already adding to the load I'm carrying. My chest pulls tighter.

Taz stands. "Give Pres a minute," he tells the brothers.

They begin to clear out, and Taz grabs a bottle of whiskey off the shelf. He places two glasses on the table and pours us each a finger. "Well, as your VP, I'm saying you fucked up. But as your mate, I'm high-fiving you cos she was fit."

I almost smile as I knock the drink back in one and hold the glass out for a second. "She was nice too," I admit. "I never understood why she did the job. I just thought she was in some kind of trouble and had to pay off a debt. I even thought about offering the club's help, but then she got reported and all contact stopped."

"What about Liv?" he asks, drinking his own and topping it up.

"She can't find out," I mutter. "She's already on the edge." I groan, burying my face in my hands. "I keep fucking it up."

"They're only coming for her because they know what she means to you," he says, his words careful as he meets my eyes.

"What are you saying?"

"If she wasn't as important, they'd find another way to get to you. One that doesn't involve her."

I shake my head. "I'm not letting her go."

"If you keep fucking up, you might not have a choice."

CHAPTER THIRTEEN

Olivia

The bed dips behind me, and Bully's arm wraps around my waist. I glance at the bedside clock, noting it's early evening. I must've dozed off. I stretch out, his hand sliding under my shirt just as I remember our fight. He nuzzles my neck, teeth grazing my skin. *Typical*. Using sex to slip back into my good books.

"I'm sorry," he whispers, and I freeze. Words like that rarely fall from his lips. "I fucked up, Liv. You're the one person I should never doubt. The one who always has my back."

I turn in his arms, narrowing my eyes. "You've found something out." His expression is innocent. *Too* innocent. "What have you discovered?" I press.

"Nothing, darlin'," he murmurs, his lips brushing my shoulder.

"Bully, I know every guilty look you've ever worn. So, out with it. Who fucked up?"

He lifts my top, trailing kisses down to my stomach. "And you were right earlier," he murmurs. "It's your role to run the whores. I shouldn't have interfered. The rota stays. I'll deal with Poison."

Now, I'm really suspicious. "You're scaring me," I whisper.

His lips pause. "It's club business," he says gently. "But now I know, I can fix it. I can focus on us again." He smiles, moving his mouth across my chest.

"Can things be resolved with the Scorpions?" I ask.

He hums against my skin. "Yes."

I exhale, loosening my grip on the fear rising in me. "No more bloodshed?" He doesn't answer, just continues kissing. I tug his hair, forcing him to meet my eyes. "Bully, is this over?"

The sudden pop of a sharp sound cuts through the air.

He goes still.

Another pop.

This time, he's off the bed in an instant. "Stay here. Don't leave this room," he orders.

"What's going on?" Another crack splits the air. "Bully, that's the same sound I heard at the bar. Is it gunfire?" My voice shakes.

He grabs my shoulders, firm but steady. "Olivia, focus." I breathe in, out. "Stay here. No matter what."

"But Bria . . . what about my sister?"

"I'll find her."

He's out the door before I can speak again. My legs carry me to the doorway, breath catching in my throat. I can't stay here. I have to find Bria.

The club is shaking from the commotion below, the voices barking orders, the unmistakable thud of boots on the stairs. But all I can think of is Bria. I slip out the bedroom, careful to avoid the creaking board near the railing, and edge toward the back stairs.

My heart thuds in my chest as I ease myself down each step, my back pressed to the wall. If I can make it out and around the back, Bria will probably be under the tree where she said she was going to read.

"Liv."

The voice stops me cold.

Dagger steps from the shadows, his presence as smooth and poisonous as his name. He's calm, *too calm,* like the chaos doesn't touch him. "You need to hide," he whispers, glancing around. "Now."

"My sister . . ."

"Is hiding too. Fuck. Why are you so damn perfect, always looking out for someone? Who will save you, though, Liv?"

I swallow, backing up a step. "What's going on?"

"Just a little fun."

I almost choke on my words. "Fun?" I hiss. "This isn't fun, Darren. Why can't you both just fucking stop this bullshit?"

He grins easy, like I'm the one being hysterical. "Three things that men fight over, Liv—money, power, and pussy. Which one do you think it is?"

"Bully thinks it's me," I whisper, my eyes reaching his.

He smirks, his hand lifting but pausing when I flinch. Slowly, deliberately, he cups my face. I freeze. His touch is soft, but it feels like poison sinking beneath my skin. "Of course, he blames you. That's the kind of man he is."

"So, it's not me?"

"You're cute," he murmurs. "Just say the word and I'll get you out of here. I can give you more. The world, even. But this?" His eyes glint, sharp and unforgiving. "This isn't about you, mama. This is all him." He moves closer until he's on the same step, towering over me.

"Why?" I whisper, my breaths coming out hard as he continues to stare deep into my soul.

"Because of Lila."

My blood runs cold. "Who's Lila?"

"Ask him, Liv. Ask your old man all about Lila Carson." He leans in, brushing a kiss over my lips, quick, deliberate, *wrong*. Then he turns away. "Now, go upstairs like a good girl," he calls over his shoulder, "and don't come out until I've gone."

I back up, taking each step carefully but watching the space where he was. I get to the top, and the sound of gunfire stops. I hold my breath. Waiting. Listening. There's nothing. I step onto the landing as heavy boots run up the stairs, and I freeze, sagging with relief when Bully appears. His eyes narrow. "What are you doing out here?"

I smile, too relieved to care about his snappy tone as I throw my arms around him. "Are you okay?"

He holds me too, his face buried into my neck as he inhales deeply. "Everyone's fine."

"Good," I whisper. I run my hands over his face, tears stinging my eyes. "Good."

He looks amused. "Are you okay?"

I nod a little too quickly as a tear escapes down my cheek. "Who's Lila Carson?" His sharp intake of breath is so loud against the silence, it takes me by surprise. "Who is she, Bully?" But I know. Deep down, I already know that whatever his answer is, I won't like it. *It's going to break us.*

"Where did you hear that name?" he asks, removing my hands from his face and holding me at arm's length. "Where, Liv?" he suddenly snaps, shaking me.

"Oh god," I whisper as pain squeezes my heart. My hands go to my mouth as more tears escape. "You did it again."

"Who told you about her?" he demands.

"Dagger," I say, barely a whisper. My smile is sad, my heart breaking. "Dagger told me."

"Pres, we need you down here," calls Boss, breaking the tension between us.

Bully lunges for me, grabbing my upper arm and dragging me towards the bedroom. "Stay in there until I come back. Don't fucking move."

I can't stop my sobs as they leave me, painful and loud. "If you leave me now, without an explanation, I'm walking out of here."

"No," he says firmly. "You're not going anywhere." And he slams the bedroom door shut, locking it.

I fall onto the bed, crying into the pillows.

Bully

Downstairs is chaos. Furniture is tipped up, bullets lodged into anything wooden. The windows have all gone, now shattered across the floor, twinkling in the low sun like cruel little stars. The air tastes scorched, and there's a faint hum in my ears, adrenaline or maybe the echo of gunfire still vibrating off the walls.

"Have you checked in with the women?" I ask, scanning the room for any movement. Boss nods.

"All accounted for. No injuries. Is Liv okay?"

I nod, though my head is pounding. Not from a blow, just pressure, noise, too many thoughts crowding into one skull. I've got so many damn questions, and none of them have answers. *Not yet.*

Taz kicks a chunk of splintered table across the floor. It skitters to a stop against the bar. "Shooting up the front of the club," he mutters, brow furrowed, "it makes no sense. Why not force their way in? They must've realised we were unarmed when we didn't fire back."

His voice cuts through the ringing in my ears. The logic of it all doesn't hold, but then it hits me, cold and sharp. "It was a distraction," I say, the words sticking in my throat. "He wanted to talk to Liv."

Silence drops like a weight. Boss shifts beside me as Taz looks up sharply.

"You think he . . . Dagger used all this just to get to her?"

I nod slowly. "She knows," I add, "about Lila."

There's a beat before anyone speaks. Dust dances in the sunlight, drifting through the blown-out windows like ghosts. The kind that don't rest easy. "Shit. You think he got to her in our own damn clubhouse?" mutters Taz. The thought he was so close to her . . . *again.* I shudder. *Fuck.* I turn and head for the stairs. I need answers. *Now.*

The door unlocks with a soft click, and I push it open like I'm stepping into a warzone.

Because I am.

Liv's standing by the bed, stuffing clothes into a duffel, her face blotchy and red, eyes hollowed out like something's already died in her. Something I killed. She freezes when she sees me. Not in fear . . . in fury.

"Liv," I say, voice low. "What are you doing?"

"What does it look like?" she snaps, zipping the bag closed like it's final. Like *we're* final.

My chest tightens. "Put it down."

"No."

She's not crying anymore. This might be worse. The tears I can handle, but this silence, this steel . . . it terrifies me.

"Don't do this," I say. "Not like this." I take a step towards her, but she flinches back like I've raised a hand. "I was going to tell you," I say. "After all this, after tonight—"

"Bullshit. We've been here before, Bully." Her lips tremble, but she doesn't cry. "You always do this. You tell me the truth too late, when I can't unhear it. When I'm already bleeding from it."

"I can fix it."

"Who is she?" she demands.

"She worked in the prison . . . on my wing."

She pauses, her brow furrowing as she works it out, and then her eyes find me again, and the fury is replaced with hurt. "The one time I didn't worry, and you were fucking someone on the inside? What was she, a cleaner? A visitor?" I shake my head, placing my hands on my hips. "Then who was she, Bully?" she screams, her face red with anger.

"A screw," I mutter, breaking eye contact. "She worked the wing."

Her sharp intake of breath is like another punch to the gut. "How is that possible?" Her words are low, barely a whisper.

"It happens more than you think," I say, unhelpfully, and she screams in frustration, barrelling towards me like a woman possessed, raining blows against my chest with tight fists. "It was a mistake," I repeat, trying to grab her wrists as her arms flail around, catching me on my cheek. When I finally grab her, she stills, her eyes burning into me like she's trying to convey all her hatred in that one look.

Her chest heaves with exertion, and she pulls free, stepping back. "How many times do you get to call it a mistake before it's a pattern?"

I shake my head, swallowing hard. "I was weak. I let her in when I should've kept my head down. It was hardly a thing at all before she got found out. She got fired, Liv. She lost everything."

"Oh, poor her. Should I feel sorry for her?" she asks, her voice thick with sarcasm.

"Then she took her own life. And Dagger . . . he was her husband. But I didn't know any of that until today."

Realisation passes over her face. "I knew you were acting odd. I asked you outright." I nod, more guilt seeping into my already saturated heart. "You had no intention of telling me at all," she whispers, her voice cracking slightly. "If you were going to, you'd have told me then . . . when I asked."

I look away. "I was scared of losing you."

"Pity you weren't scared when you were fucking Dagger's old lady."

"I didn't love her," I say. "Lila. I swear to you, Liv, I didn't. It was a mistake. A moment. A mess I made in a place where everything was already broken."

"How long?" she asks, folding her arms over her chest. "Actually, how many times?"

I shrug, swallowing the dread in my throat. "Not long."

"How many fucking times, Bully?"

I sigh heavily. "Maybe ten. Fifteen."

"Wow."

"But it meant nothing, Liv. Just sex."

"It meant everything. It meant losing me. It meant causing a war with Dagger. So, I hope she was worth it." She picks up the bag, and I immediately snatch it.

"You're not leaving me."

"Oh, I am," she says firmly. "I am leaving and I'm not coming back."

"It's not safe."

"Dagger doesn't want to hurt me. He wants to hurt you."

"And hurting you will do that. He knows that."

She scoffs. "So, why hasn't he done it already?" I don't have the answer, and after a second of silence, a cruel smirk spreads over her face. It doesn't suit her. "He's always nice to me, Bully. Like he cares."

"He doesn't care. He's using you to get to me."

"Is that why he kissed me?"

My world tilts, and I drop her bag to the floor. "What did you say?"

She grins now, like she's enjoying my pain. "On the stairs. He kissed me. It was quick. Deliberate. Wrong. Just like *you*." Her words hit like fists. I stagger under the weight of them, but I deserve every single one. "And do you know what? I wasn't mad about it. In fact, it felt . . . nice."

"Stop," I whisper.

Instead, she steps closer. "And I thought about what it would feel like to fuck him."

"Liv," I whisper, my voice dangerously low. A warning.

"Because it's only ever been you, Bully. Even when you went inside, I stayed faithful to you. And there were men," she says, smiling like it's a good memory. "Many men who tried. Many men who saw in me what you never have. I should've taken my chances. I realise that now."

"You don't mean that. You're hurting."

"Tell me, was she ever there when I visited?" I stare at the ground, the knot in my chest pulling tighter. "Was she in that big room, watching you while I visited?"

"It meant—"

"Don't you dare say it again," she screams, and I press my lips together in a tight line. "Did you laugh at me?" Her voice breaks a little, and my heart twists painfully.

"Of course not. Never."

"Was she prettier? Better in bed?"

"Jesus, Liv, of course not. But she . . ." The words trail off, and Liv swipes a stray tear away, waiting for my next words. "She was there and willing." I wince, hating how it sounds out loud.

"It's not my fault I wasn't."

"I was in a bad place, missing you and the club. She took my mind off it."

The door bursts open, and we both turn to Bria. Her face is pale, and she's clutching her mobile phone tightly. When she sees me, then the bag, she thrusts the phone at Liv. "Press play," she says, glaring at me with hatred.

CHAPTER FOURTEEN

Olivia

I take the mobile, but I already know by the way Bria's eyes are fixed on Bully that she's angry. And this video is why.

My thumb trembles as I press play. I sink onto the edge of the bed, barely breathing, as the unmistakable sound of breathy moans fills the room.

My frown deepens as the image sharpens. *Them.* Bully. Lila.

"I love you," she whispers.

Bully steps forward. "Liv, what are you watching?" His voice is tight. He already knows. He's heard that voice before.

I glance back at the screen just in time to see him yank her hair, turning her face toward the camera. Whoever is filming moves closer. She's not shocked. She smiles for the camera.She *knows* she's being filmed.

"Say it back," she pants, dragging Bully's mouth to hers. They kiss, and my stomach turns. My heart caves in. It's passionate, hungry.

"Bitch needs her mouth filled," the man behind the camera says with a laugh.

The screen goes black. Bully exhales, relieved it's finished.

"It's not over," Bria says flatly as another video starts to play.

This time, Bully is asleep. Peaceful. Vulnerable. The camera pans slowly as Lila strips, tossing her clothes to the floor.

I knew she'd be beautiful. Somehow, that makes it *worse*. She winks at the camera.

"Liv, how is this helping?" Bully snaps. "Why would you show her this?" He rounds on Bria, his voice hot with anger. "Where did you even get it?"

"I was sent it," she says, icy calm. "It's all over the internet." Her words slice through me, knowing that others will see my humiliation.

Onscreen, Lila climbs onto Bully, grinding against his body. He stirs. His eyes open, and when he sees her, he gives a sleepy smile. *That* smile. The one he gives *me* in the morning.

"I love you," she breathes.

"I know," he says back. "Now, fuck me."

She starts to ride him, moaning. The camera wobbles as a hand reaches in, groping her.

I stop the video, and Bully drops to his knees before me, his fingers digging into my thighs like that'll somehow stop me from leaving. Bria picks up my bag. "I've already packed. I'll meet you downstairs," she says, heading out the door.

"I'll do anything to make it right," he whispers desperately.

I watch the emotions play out on his face, but I can't react. I'm *numb*. We've done this too many times. "You can't make it right," I mutter.

"I can. I told you, I've changed. Since her, there's been no one." I stand, and he wraps his arms around my legs, clinging to me. "Please don't leave me, Liv."

"Let go."

"Please, I'll do anything."

"Let. Go."

"I can't keep you safe out there, darlin'. I'm begging you, don't walk out that door. I'll give you space. I'll stay out your way."

"Let go, Liam."

He stills at that one word, and his grip loosens. He pushes to his feet, rushing to the door and blocking my path. "I've been an idiot too many times, never appreciating what I've got. But you're it for me, Liv."

I scoff. It slips out like I've lost control, and I laugh until tears fill my eyes. "I'm not *it* for you, Liam. I never was, and I've been fucking stupid to think I could change you. The truth is you don't want to change. Not for me."

"I'll prove it. Give me one more chance."

I shake my head. "No. There's been too many chances. Too many apologies. Too many pretty women you've been lost in. And I am *tired.* Tired of coming second. Tired of you making me feel like I'm not enough. So, I'm putting me first. Get out of my way or so help me, God, I will kill you with my bare hands."

He gives a wary look before stepping to one side. I push past and rush from the room, taking the stairs faster when I hear his heavy boots following.

Bria is by the door, and she offers me a sad smile as I join her, taking my bag. Taz appears, his eyes falling to the bags.

"Bria, talk some sense into her. I can't keep either of you safe outside this club," says Bully, swooping down to pick Misty up.

"We'll take our chances," snaps Bria.

I look Taz in the eyes. "I do not want this club to protect me," I say firmly. "If you put a guy on me or so much as drive by me in the street, I'll call the police and have you done for stalking."

"You know that ain't my call, Liv," he mutters, glancing to Bully.

"You realise what you're saying, Liv," Bully snaps. "You may as well sign your own death warrant."

"Goodbye, Liam," I say, not quite meeting his eyes as I give Misty a quick stroke behind the ear. I was wrong about her—she fits here perfectly.

Bria grips my hand so tightly, I fear she's cutting off my blood circulation as we rush across the car park outside. She taps away nervously on her phone to find an Uber. "You're shaking," I note.

She glances up. "Yeah, well, you never know how Bully's gonna react. He's unpredictable."

"Who sent you the video?" I ask.

"Darren. Dagger. Whatever his fucking name is."

"How did he get your number?"

"I have no idea, Liv, but I'm guessing he's just as dangerous as Loverboy and has access to whatever he needs. For the record, I get to approve all future boyfriends."

The gate slides open, and we step through it. As it slides closed again, my heart hurts that little bit more. It's final. Finished. That's when the tears really start, and Bria drops her bag, wrapping her arms around me. "Oh shit," she whispers, sounding panicked. "Don't cry, Liv. He's not worth it."

I sniffle, laughing slightly. "How many times have you said that same sentence?"

She laughs too. "Far too many."

The Uber pulls up, and Bria stuffs our bags in the boot before climbing in beside me. Luckily, I kept my apartment, which I'm thankful for. Maybe I always knew deep down I'd need it again.

Bria's light snores make me smile as the credits roll on the film we'd been watching. I lower the volume and glance at her phone. Mine's long gone, smashed by Bully in his jealous rage. I scoff. *Wanker.*

I pick it up and unlock it easily using her date-of-birth PIN. *Predictable.* I scroll through her contacts until I find it. *Dagger.*

Me: It's Liv. I'm using my sister's phone. I need to see you. Urgently.

The reply comes almost instantly.

Darren: On my way.

I stare at the screen like it might explain everything, but it doesn't.

Then I hear it a minute later—the low, unmistakable rumble of a bike. My heart leaps as I rush to the window. The orange and black kutte confirms it's Dagger, but I can't let him come up here.

I scan the street instinctively, searching for signs of a Royal Bastard tail. If they've ignored me and someone *is* watching, it won't be long before the entire club shows up.

Me: Not here.

Send.

Me: There's a bar around the corner. Meet me there.

Darren: Your rules . . . for now.

I let out a shaky breath and delete the entire conversation. But my eyes linger on one of the videos. I swallow hard and toss the phone onto the table like it's burned me. Some things you can't unsee.

I slip out quietly, careful not to wake Bria. There's no time to change. I'm still in joggers, hair twisted into a messy knot, and no makeup. *Good.* I don't want him to get the wrong idea.

The bar's dim and smells like stale beer and cheap aftershave. A few heads turn when I shove the heavy door open, but they lose interest fast. Except one. *Dagger.*

He strolls over with that arrogant smirk. "So, we meet again," he says, amused.

I brush past him without a word and take the farthest seat in the corner. He follows, lounging in the chair like it belongs to him. "What was so urgent, *mama*?" he drawls.

The nickname is irritating. The way it slides from his mouth makes my cheeks flush, and that only pisses me off more. "How did you get Bria's number?"

He shrugs. "I have my ways."

"And our address?" He grins wider. *Smug bastard.* I exhale sharply. "I've left Bully." I don't meet his eyes, just fix mine on the wall over his shoulder. "Am I safe now?"

He leans back, arms crossing over his thick chest. "Depends on what you mean by safe."

"From the Scorpions?" I snap impatiently.

Dagger tilts his head, eyes skimming over me with deliberate slowness. "You always start conversations with a demand, *mama*, or am I just special?"

I bristle. "This isn't a game."

He leans forward, forearms resting on the table, the weight of his gaze pressing down on me. "That's where you're wrong. It's *exactly* a game. And every player has their role." He smiles, slow, wolfish. "Even you."

"I just want to be left alone. I want Bria safe."

He doesn't respond right away. Instead, his eyes drop to my mouth then slowly trail down my body, lingering like he's letting himself imagine what I'd look like under him. He doesn't hide it, and I hate the heat that creeps up my neck in response. "Tell me something, Liv . . ." His voice lowers, velvet dirty. "You come running to me in joggers, no makeup, hair a mess . . . was that your version of playing hard to get? Or are you just trying to convince me you're not here to be fucked?"

"I'm not," I say, but it comes out too fast, too defensive.

He grins like he already knows the truth. "Screwing you while I'm burning your ex's world to the ground could get messy." He leans in, voice barely a whisper now. "But messy doesn't scare me."

I swallow hard and shift in my seat. "This isn't about sex."

"Everything's about sex." His grin vanishes. "Or revenge. Sometimes both."

I shake my head. "You're not going to give me a straight answer, are you?"

He shrugs. "You and Bria? Safe for now. But you're standing in a war zone, Liv. The Royal Bastards made this personal. Bully made it lethal."

"Why did you send Bria that video?"

His expression darkens, like a storm is creeping in behind his eyes. "Why do you think?"

"To punish me?"

He leans back again, the confidence oozing from his every pore. "If I wanted to punish you, I have more creative ways." His eyes look almost black as he fixes me with a heated stare. "Just say the word."

I clear my throat, glancing around to see if anyone else can feel the hot tension pinging around the room. "By leaving Bully, I've removed myself from the game. No?"

Dagger doesn't even blink. "It doesn't work like that, mama."

"Then tell me how it works," I snap. "Because you've had plenty of chances to kill me and haven't, so I'm guessing you don't want me dead."

A slow smirk curves across his mouth. "Everyone is where I've *allowed* them to be in my game. Including you. I want your man to suffer for what he did."

My jaw tightens. "This is all a little too dramatic, don't you think? Couples break up all the time. People cheat. Declaring war because Lila got freaky at work screams *crazy*."

I don't see his hand coming, just feel it, lightning-fast and iron-tight around my throat. In one effortless motion, he drags me towards him across the table, until our faces are so close, I can feel the heat of his breath. "You're alive," he growls, voice low and venomous, "because I've *allowed* it. And I can take that order back any second."

My hands scramble around his wrist, nails digging in, but he doesn't loosen his grip. "What my men have planned for you," he leans in farther, his lips brushing my cheek, "is so much worse than you can imagine."

He holds me there a moment longer, long enough for the panic to hit, for my lungs to beg for breath, then shoves me back. I stumble into the seat, gasping. My hands instinctively fly to my neck, fingers rubbing where his grip burned hot. My chest heaves as my heart thunders wildly. He watches me like nothing happened, like that sort of interaction should be normal to me. "Bully will suffer," he says calmly. "And if *you* want to survive this, you'll remember exactly who the fuck you're talking to."

My throat burns. My lungs scream. But I force myself to breathe slow, to lift my chin. He wants me afraid, wants me crawling, but I've lived with Bully. I know what fear feels like, and this isn't it.

I meet Dagger's eyes, steady now. "If you really wanted me dead," I rasp, "you wouldn't have bothered grabbing my throat. You'd have let your men do it in some alley and left my body as a message." He says nothing, but I see the flicker of interest in his expression. "You didn't come here to kill me," I continue, "but you were waiting for my call." I narrow my eyes thoughtfully. "Close by. You knew I was home. You knew I'd left Bully." He grins, enjoying how I'm putting the pieces together. "You're following me." He doesn't deny it. "You like me." It's a risky guess, but again, he doesn't deny that either, just watches me with intrigue. "And you haven't sent your men because you can't trust them around me, which means I'm something to you."

Without a word, he rises to his feet. "Watch your back, mama." He heads for the door. "The board's getting bloody."

Bully

Silence.

It stretches out, wrapping around my ribs like barbed wire. Every second she's gone, the tighter it pulls. I stare at the space where she stood, chest rising hard, fists clenched. Taz shifts beside me, but I can't look at him. Can't look at anyone. I've lost her, for real.

This isn't some fight where she storms off and cools down at Bria's. Not a night at her sister's, ignoring my calls. *This* is final. She didn't cry. She didn't break. She left.

And she called me *Liam.*

The sound of my name in her voice like that, it gutted me. Cold. Sharp. Like she'd already buried me.

I drag a hand down my face, sucking in a breath that does nothing to clear the burning behind my eyes. Then I spin, grab the nearest chair, and launch it across the room. It splinters against the wall. Taz flinches but doesn't say shit.

I stalk across the room, throwing open the cupboard behind the bar and knocking bottles out until I find the one I'm looking for. Half-full whiskey. *Expensive.* Saved for celebrations or funerals. *This feels like the latter.*

I twist the cap, take a swig straight from the bottle, and let the fire settle in my gut. It's not enough.

"She's got no fuckin' clue what she's walking into," I mutter, pacing again. "Dagger's out there, Scorpions are watching, and she just handed herself over like a goddamn gift."

"She's scared, man," Taz says quietly. "And you, what you did . . . that video . . ."

I round on him. "Don't."

He holds his hands up, but his eyes are steady. "You can't undo it. You think she's coming back? After that?"

I shove past him, furious at him, furious at myself. I grab a vodka bottle and throw it across the room. Glass shatters and liquid drips down the wall like blood. "She was *mine*," I growl.

"You want her safe?" he asks. "Then let her go. You send someone after her, she'll hate you more. You let her breathe, maybe she'll remember what's good in you."

I stare at the mess on the floor. The broken glass. The empty doorway. I shake my head. "She won't. Not this time." Then, quieter, I mutter, "Not after what she saw."

A long silence stretches between us. Taz doesn't press. He just stands there, letting me drown in it. And I do, because there's nothing left to hold on to. Except the rage . . . and *revenge.*

"We hit back," I say firmly.

"Wait, Pres, you're not thinking straight."

"Everything is pretty fucking clear, Taz. He sent that video to break us apart. A job well done. Now, we hit back. *Harder*. It's time for the games to end. I want blood."

"You should call Jameson," he mutters. "Run all this by him first."

"Already have," I mutter, "and he agrees with me. It's time we stop dancing around those fuckers and hit back." I head for church. "Gather everyone. We need a plan."

I don't sit. I *pace*. Restless. Wound tight like a ticking bomb with no off switch. She's *gone*, and Dagger's out there licking his lips like this is his opening. I slam my fist on the long table. Over my dead fuckin' body.

My brothers begin to filter in, all taking their seats, and I get straight to the point. "They've got a shipment coming in tomorrow," I say. "It's heavy with drugs, telling me they plan on supplying over county lines too." I lay out a map in the centre of the table marked with their planned journey. "They have lorries coming in at Immingham. Two lorries, each listed as carrying car parts. They'll get off the boat around three p.m. and are expected to sail through border control. From there, they'll head this way," I tell them, trailing my finger along the planned route. "They'll end up at Colwick Industrial Estate around six-ish."

"Why ain't they splitting it across the country?" asks Brains.

I shrug. "Maybe they could only get two lorries through without raising questions. Either way, their place in Colwick is away from prying eyes. I expect they'll split the shipment and have smaller vehicles collect overnight." I take a breath. "But that doesn't matter, cos we'll be cutting off their supply. I want them dead before their boots hit the ground."

Mad Dog grins, eyes lighting up. "Thought we were waiting."

"We *were*," I snap, "until they started playing dirty. Now, I want them to realise who the fuck they've messed with. No more warning shots. The war has started, and I won't rest until I've wiped them out."

Taz shifts in his seat, arms folded. "You think they'll use Liv some more?"

My jaw flexes as that knot in my chest twists. "Him sending the video was only the start."

"Then we take the fight to them," Boss mutters.

"No." I grab the map off the table, scrunching it. "We *cripple* them. Burn their supply. Cut their legs out before they can run."

I lay out another map, this one showing the industrial estate. "Two entry points here. Only one CCTV blind spot. We roll in heavy, three cars, five riders. No colours. No mercy."

"Shoot first?" Ragnar asks.

"Don't stop shooting," I growl. "We leave no bodies to identify. Strip the patches. Burn the gear. Make it look like a deal gone wrong."

Mad Dog's practically vibrating. "What about the product?"

"We torch it."

A beat of silence follows. Taz frowns. "You sure, Pres? We can move it quickly."

"I don't give a fuck about cash. This is about sending a message." My voice drops low. "Dagger thinks I'm off my game. Thinks I'm distracted. So, let's show him what I look like when I've got nothing left to lose."

CHAPTER FIFTEEN

Olivia

I open my new phone and turn it on. Bria watches me through intrigued eyes as I slot the new SIM card in. "Tell me again," she pushes, crossing her legs and sitting straighter.

I sigh. "I just needed to hear it from his mouth."

"And he said we're safe?" she clarifies.

"Yes," I mutter, the half lie almost choking me. "So, we can relax. Maybe just keep your eyes peeled for the Bastards."

"I find it weird Bully hasn't come looking, don't you?"

I shrug, avoiding her eyes. The truth is, I find his silence worrying. "He's got the message. I couldn't have said it clearer."

"And you're really done with him?"

"Yes," I hiss.

"It doesn't feel like it."

I glance up to find her still watching me. "What do you mean?"

"You and Bully are addicted to each other. Fucking. Fighting. It's become a game."

Her words spark something, something from last night with Dagger, and I sit straighter. "None of this is a game," I snap. "Yet the men seem to think so. And I was never any good at playing games, especially when I didn't know the rules. So, we're making up our own rules now. Fuck Dagger and fuck Bully."

"Are you going back to work?" she asks.

I nod. "It's why I need my phone, so we can keep checking in."

Her eyes narrow suspiciously. "If we're safe now, why do I need to check in?"

I can't tell her I think Dagger is stalking me. She'll panic and run right back to Bully. And so, I force a smile as I stand. "Because we're sisters, Bria." And I head for the door.

Ann embraces me the second I walk through the door. "I've missed you."

I smile, holding her a little longer than needed because she makes me feel so loved, and right now, I need it. "I missed you too. And the pups, of course." I shrug from my coat. "How are things?"

"We've finally rehomed Dodger," she says excitedly, and I clap my hands together with happiness. Dodger was another old dog we'd had here for over three years.

The door opens, and a woman enters carrying a huge bunch of white roses. I almost roll my eyes at his cliché as she puts them on the side. "These are for Liv," she states, and I force a smile as I step closer to sign her clipboard.

"Thanks."

"Who's a lucky girl?" asks Ann, grinning as she takes a sniff.

"Keep them on reception," I mutter. "I don't want them." I head to the back room to dump my coat and bag, and then I open the card.

'Mama, I hear you like white because red reminds you of blood. I'm sorry for losing it yesterday. It's a tense time. Forgive me. D x'

My brow furrows. There's only one man who calls me mama, and it isn't Bully. But how the hell does Dagger know my preference and the reason why? I stuff the card in my back pocket and head back out to Ann. I've taken so much time off already, I refuse to spend it thinking about either of those men.

By five o' clock, I'm exhausted. I promised Ann I'd lock up, so she left early, but I didn't anticipate having a mad rush on for the last hour.

I lock the door and turn right as a motorbike rolls to a stop. I groan when Bully steps off. "I know you don't want to speak to me," he begins. I don't, but a small part of me is relieved to see him, like having him nearby makes me safer. I glance around, wondering if Dagger is watching.

"What do you want?"

"Just checking in to see if you're okay," he says, not quite meeting my eyes.

"I'm good," I snap, throwing my bag on my shoulder and heading in the direction of home. I almost smile when I hear his boots following. He doesn't speak, just follows. And when I get to my apartment block, he waits a few steps behind, watching as I go inside. When I turn back, he's gone.

Bully

The rain's a fine mist, clinging to leather and metal. Our headlights stay off as we roll in, slow and silent, like wolves circling the kill.

Two lorries sit parked in the middle of the site. Engines off. Lights out. No signage. No logos. But I know what's underneath the crates of car parts in those trailers. Coke. Kilos of it. Pure and heavy.

We move around the containers like stealth lions on a kill mission. Black hoodies. Gloves. Suppressors already locked and loaded.

Mad Dog eyes the scene. "Two drivers, three unloaders. Five total."

"Then we make it fast," I mutter.

We fan out. I move left, circling behind the first lorry. Boss and Smiler sweep wide. Taz and Mad Dog approach straight-on. Five shadows in a death waltz.

One of the unloaders lights a cigarette, laughing about something. *First shot.* Taz takes out the smoker. Silent. Swift. The man drops mid-laugh.

Confusion erupts too slow to matter. The second unloader reaches for his weapon, but Mad Dog plugs him twice in the chest before he even clears leather.

I charge the cab of the first lorry and rip the door open. The driver inside barely has time to flinch before I pull the trigger point-blank. Blood sprays the windshield.

His partner scrambles in the other cab, trying to start the engine, but Boss is already there.He yanks the door open and drags him out kicking and screaming. Smiler slams him into the concrete, pressing the muzzle of his Glock to the guy's eye. "Beg."

The man opens his mouth . . . *Bang*. His skull cracks like a melon. It's followed by silence, except for the sound of blood hitting pavement and the hiss of cooling engines.

I climb into the back of the first trailer. Just like the intel said, crates of brake pads, discs, springs. Fake manifests tucked into clipboards. But beneath the fourth row, there it is, plastic-wrapped bricks. Kilos.

White gold. I tear one open, dip a pinkie, and rub it on my gums. "Pure," I mutter.

Taz joins me. "We could move this. It's easy money."

"We didn't come for cash," I remind him. I jump down, nodding at Boss and Mad Dog. "Soak it."

They move fast, cracking open petrol cans. The stink hits hard. Smiler drags the bodies into a pile, and Mad Dog sets the final match. It goes up with a loud whoosh, causing us all to flinch back. Flames roar, lighting the night orange and gold. The second lorry follows.

We stand back and watch it burn, faces lit by fire and fury. A funeral for Dagger's profits. A message written in blood and smoke.

Boss spits. "Think he'll get it?"

I smile, cold, tight. "He'll get it."

Because this wasn't just business.

This was personal.

Olivia

I don't think much about it when Bria insists we go for a few drinks at the local on the corner. Mainly because it's something we'd always do before Bully was released, and I've slipped back into my old life easily. Even with the threat of Dagger hanging over me, I'm confident he doesn't plan on hurting me.

We're two drinks in when he approaches the table. Bria spots him first, and the way she stiffens warns me of his arrival before I actually meet his eyes. "You didn't like the roses, mama?" he asks, placing a hand loosely over his heart to feign hurt. "Maybe you'll let me buy your next drink," he suggests. "Lemon gin, yes?"

My blood runs cold. There's no way this is coincidence. How does he know all this stuff? Bria must be thinking the same because I feel her gaze burning into me, but I don't break eye contact with him. He needs to see I'm not rattled by his sudden appearance. *Again*.

"Actually, I hate lemons. And white roses remind me of Bully. He once laid me on a bed of white rose petals," I say, smiling like I'm enjoying the memory. "Right before he took my virginity." His gaze turns steely. "Oh, I'm sorry, I assumed you knew everything about me," I say innocently.

"Walk me out," he says firmly, right as the girls arrive. Bria gets swept up in hugs, so I silently slide away from the table and head out with Dagger. "You think you're funny taunting me?"

"No. Not at all," I snap, stopping outside the bar. It's busy with people standing around smoking, so I'm not worried as he turns to face me. He backs me to the wall, and I keep my breathing steady even though my heart begins to race.

He places a hand right above my head, caging me in as his face moves closer to mine. "He isn't giving up," he whispers, his breath tickling the wispy hairs that frame my face. "Walking you home like that."

"What do you want from me, Dagger?"

"I want you to understand," he tells me. "To see what kind of a man he is."

"Why is that so important to you?"

"You're his weakness, Liv. If I take you, I hurt him."

"I've already left him," I cry. "What more do you want?"

His phone rings out, and he answers, keeping his eyes fixed on me. "Yeah?" His body stills.

Then his entire expression shifts. "How the *fuck* would they know?" The venom in his voice is so sharp, it cuts the air. He ends the call and pockets the phone with a clenched jaw, bracing his other hand above my head, fully caging me now.

His voice is tight when he says, "Seems he's fighting back."

"What does that mean?" I ask, but my stomach already knows. There's something ugly rolling in the distance. I can *feel* it.

Then, a shrieking whistle through the air.

Something slams into the wall above us and explodes in shards of glass. I scream, and he grabs me, his arm locking around my waist as he throws us both down.

We hit the pavement hard. Dagger's body covers mine, his arm protectively over my head, glass raining like knives around us.

Gunshots, sharp and savage, rip through the air. I choke on my breath, my arms curling over my head as my ears ring.

"Bria," I gasp, heart splitting.

"She's inside," he mutters, his mouth by my ear. "She'll be safe."

More bullets tear through the air. Screams, chaos, people running. Tires squeal on asphalt. Dagger's grip tightens, and I feel the heat of him, the rage simmering just beneath his calm.

I twist beneath him. "This is your war. I'm not supposed to be in it."

He meets my eyes, deadly calm. "You've been in it since the moment he fucked my wife."

A spray of gunfire hits the car parked nearby, and sparks fly as metal is torn apart.

"We have to move," he growls. "*Now.*"

Dagger moves fast, fluid, yanking me to my feet with a grip that bruises. "Stay low," he snaps, shoving me against him as he twists us between two parked cars. More shots crack overhead and screams pierce the air as people scatter.

"We're gonna make a move," he tells me. "Around the back of the bar. We can get inside there." He looks out from behind the cars. "One," he growls, and I tighten my grip. "Two." A pause. "*Three.*"

We make a run for it, reaching the empty beer garden, now abandoned in the chaos. Dagger pulls the back door open and shoves me inside. "Bria," I scream, looking around at the groups of people huddled together, ducked down behind tables. She stands, and I breathe a sigh of relief.

Tyres can be heard outside, screeching away, followed closely by sirens. Dagger spins me to face him. "We need to get out of here."

"No way," I say, taking Bria's hand.

"Your man killed three of mine tonight," he hisses close to my ear. "And then he came here to try and get me . . . or you."

"Bully wouldn't come for me," I snap.

"What if he saw us together, mama? What if that sent him over the edge? You're not safe out here." My throat tightens as blue lights illuminate the bar. "I can keep you safe."

"No," says Bria, holding me back. "We don't even know you."

"Liv," he says, holding out a hand.

My mind is racing as adrenaline surges around my body. "You should get out of here," I almost whisper. "Before they come in and start asking questions."

CHAPTER SIXTEEN

Bully

My mobile buzzes across the dresser, bringing me from my sleep. I grab it blindly, not bothering to open my eyes. "Huh?"

"Bully, it's Mark Taylor." I frown, pushing to sit up. He's a police officer my uncle had on the payroll for years. I glance at my phone to check the time. One a.m. "I thought you should know The Woodthorpe was shot up tonight." He pauses a beat before adding, "Your old lady was there."

I dive from the bed, holding the phone between my ear and shoulder as I tug my jeans on. "Is she okay?"

"She's fine, just a bit shook up. Said she didn't see anything cos she was inside. There were casualties, Bully. Too many."

"Do you know who was behind it?"

"No. There're turf wars kicking off every damn day at the minute."

"Yeah?"

"You wouldn't know anything about coke flooding in?"

I pause, running my fingers through my hair. "I can tell you there's been a chink in the chain of supply, so you'll see it drying up for a short time. Longer if I have my way."

"Good to know, Bully. Keep up the good work." And he disconnects.

Taz and Smiler are less than impressed when I drag their arses out of bed. Taz joins us in my office still rubbing the sleep from his eyes. "The one night I decide to get my head down early and you wake me at," he checks his watch, "quarter past one in the morning." He yawns as he sits beside Smiler.

"The Woodthorpe was shot up tonight. Liv was there." Taz mutters a string of curses, and I hold up my hand to stop him. "She's fine. Just shaken up."

"Those fuckers," hisses Smiler.

"It would've been around the time of our own little destruction job, which means at that point they didn't know anything."

"So, it wasn't a retaliation for that," Taz states. "Meaning they're coming back at us daily, not bothering if we retaliate or not."

"I need to see Liv. Check she's okay for myself. I want you to get Whizz outta bed too and see what you can find out about tonight."

"Pres, you can't go out alone. He'll be waiting," says Taz firmly.

"I can't not go and see my old lady," I snap.

"It's obvious they knew she was there. And it's obvious your next move would be to rush to her side. A job you'd do alone, with no protection." I think over his words. "Take Smiler. Go in the back. They'll expect you to have your guard down, so they'll be watching the front."

I head over to the safe and put in the code then take out a set of keys and a new mobile phone. "I'm gonna try to send her to the safe house."

Taz smirks. "Good luck with that."

Getting around the back of Liv's apartment block isn't an easy task. We have to park the bikes three streets away and climb over fences, trailing through back gardens until we come to the six-foot wall. Smiler gives me a foot up. "I'll wait out here, I'll call if I see anything," he mutters.

I tap on the service door, and the security opens it. I slip him the hundred Taz promised him when he called ahead to get me access.

Using the stairs to get to her apartment, I lightly tap on the door. When she doesn't answer, I take out the key I had cut for emergencies like this and let myself in.

The first door I come to is already slightly ajar, and I peek in to see Bria sleeping soundly. I move to the next, carefully opening it and stepping inside. Liv is wearing one of my shirts, curled in a ball in the centre of the bed with her sheets screwed up at her feet. I smile, looking around the room at the girly décor. I remember her telling me about it when she came to visit me. She was so excited when she got this place.

I notice a card laying face down beside her phone, and I pick it up.

'Mama, I hear you like white because red reminds you of blood. I'm sorry for losing it yesterday. It's a tense time. Forgive me. D x'

I stare at the words. They don't make sense, so I read them again slower. They burn a new kind of rage deep in my gut. *Mama.* He calls *my* old lady 'mama'. My jaw is tense as I read it a third time, each word slapping a little harder than before. *Forgive him for what?* This card implies he's a lot fucking closer than she let on. How else would he know about her hatred for red roses? These are things I share with her, things only I should know. Heat floods my chest. It's not just anger burning away anymore but jealousy, sour and hot, threatening to bubble over and burn Liv if I don't rein it in.

I drop the card on the side and pick up her mobile phone, taking it and heading back into the living room. I take a seat on the couch and open it.

The only messages in her phone are from him. And he's not saved under Dagger or even Darren. D. *Fucking D*. Nicknames for one another like it's a fucking love story.

I read through the first couple of him checking in on her. Another thanking her for meeting him and reiterating what he said on the card, that he's sorry for losing it.

Then the ones from tonight. More urgent. More desperate.

> **D: Mama, are you okay? Just let me know you're safe.**

Within the same minute she replies.

> **Liv: I'm fine.**

> **D: Did you talk to the police?**

> **Liv: I'm not stupid.**

> **D: You wouldn't want to drop your old man in the shit.**

I frown. He can't be referring to himself, which means he's blaming the gunfire on *me*.

> **Liv: It's not that. I told you, I'm not getting involved in your war.**

> **D: He could've killed you tonight, mama. Meet me.**

> **Liv: I can't. Bria is on one.**

> **D: I need to see you're okay.**

> **Liv: I told you, I'm fine. Goodnight. And thanks for saving me tonight . . . again.**

> **D: Having you beneath me like that . . . got me thinking shit I shouldn't. Until next time xx**

I stare at the exchange. The fire in my chest seems lighter, dimmer. Her words take away all hope I had of ever sorting things out between us.

I go back into her bedroom. She's turned on her back now, her hands laying either side of her head, relaxed, calm. I put the mobile back and shrug from my kutte, placing it carefully on the end of her bed. Then I lean close to her ear. "Wake up," I whisper coldly, and she stirs. "Olivia," I snap more harshly, and her eyes shoot open. I slam my hand over her mouth before she can scream and force her to look at me. "You've been lying to me." Her eyes are wide with fear as they search my face for answers. I shove her away, standing and putting distance between us.

She scrambles back until she's over the other side of the bed, where she brings her knees to her chest and watches me through guarded eyes. "What do you want?"

I pick the card up and throw it at her feet. She makes no move to grab it. "Mama?" I ask, arching a brow. "He has a *nickname* for you." I take a seat by the window, keeping my eyes fixed to hers. "And now you think I'm here to hurt you." The realisation hits me hard, and I fight the urge to hold her, to reassure her.

"How did you get in here?" I don't bother to reply, even though it's on the tip of my tongue to remind her I will always be able to get to her.

"I assume there were flowers attached to that card?"

She glances at the card. "You're making something out of nothing." Her voice is quiet but steady. "He left a card. I didn't ask for it."

"And does he call you '*mama*' to your face or just when he leaves you love notes?"

She glances at her phone, which instantly annoys me. "Call him," I say coldly. "Get him here."

She waits a beat before sighing heavily, like this entire conversation is an inconvenience to her. "You wanna ask me something, ask me."

"Are you screwing him?"

"No."

"Why are you meeting up with him?"

"Because you screwed his old lady and put me in danger. It was damage limitation, trying to stop it bleeding into me and Bria."

My eyes narrow in irritation. "So, you're befriending him? You feel sorry for him?"

"No," she snaps. "I needed to know if me leaving you, leaving the club, means I'm safe."

I smirk. "And what was his answer?"

She looks away briefly. "He didn't really give me one."

I laugh. "Let me get this straight, Liv. You willingly arranged to meet a dangerous man, one who wants to get to me by using you, and you told him you were no longer under my protection." She fidgets uncomfortably, and I imagine the blush burning her cheeks, one I can't see in the dimness of the moonlight. "Clever."

"I'm still here, aren't I?" she snaps. "No thanks to your bloody club."

I frown. "Now, you trust his word?" My voice drops to a dangerous level. "He tells you my club was responsible for that shitshow, and you believe him?"

"He was there—"

I push to my feet, and she slams her lips closed. "Yes, I know. Protecting you from a threat he arranged."

I let my words sink in, and she shakes her head. "Why would he—"

"Oh, Jesus, Liv, wake up. What better way to get at me than to take what's mine? He gets you to trust him, and then he'll parade you around on his arm just to piss me off."

"Only I'm not yours."

"The result will still be the same," I mutter bitterly.

She buries her face in her hands. "You realise none of this would be happening if you just kept your dick in your pants for once."

Her words twist my already aching heart. "Yes," I whisper. "But it's done. I can't change it now. You need to stay away from him, Liv."

"I can't," she mutters. I brace myself for her next words, like she's about to confess her undying love for my enemy. "I think he's stalking me."

It's not what I expected, and I sit back down, my brow furrowed. "What?"

"He knows where I am. He knows things about me that he shouldn't . . . like the roses. How does he know that?"

"Maybe you told him?" I suggest.

"I didn't. We haven't been having meaningful chats, Bully."

"Maybe he's tracking your phone?" My mind races for an explanation.

She shakes her head. "You smashed the old one. This one's new."

I nod thoughtfully. "I'll talk to Whizz, see what he can come up with." I step closer, and she watches through mistrusting eyes. It's another reminder that I've hurt her. "Are you okay, after The Woodthorpe?" She nods, her eyes fixed to my hand as I move it closer and brush her hair away from her face. Her eyes flutter closed, and she leans into the touch like she's missing me just as much as I'm missing her. "Please avoid him until I have an answer for you. If he's stalking you, who knows what he's planning."

"If security is letting people up, how am I going to stay safe?"

"I'll speak to them." I lean down swiftly, placing a chaste kiss on her forehead and head for the door.

"You're not demanding I come back to the clubhouse?"

I glance back and almost smile at the confusion on her face. "It's another fight that neither of us need. I love you, Liv, but I know I've messed everything up. I respect your need to be here, away from me. But you know the club is your home, and you're welcome there anytime. There's a safehouse," I shrug, "you just need to ask."

Olivia

I stare after him with a mixture of confusion. If he'd demanded I go to the clubhouse, I would have refused. I'd have fought him every step. But secretly, I would have felt safer there. He's giving me space, respecting my boundaries. *But, fuck, Bully, it's the one time I need you to pull your alpha bullshit.*

I get back into bed and fall into a restless sleep.

It's Bria who wakes me a few hours later, shaking me hard. "You were sleeping heavy," she whispers, smiling when I open my eyes.

I roll onto my back. "What time is it?"

"Ten. Bully's here."

I sit up quickly. "What?"

There's a smile pulling at her lips, and I sense she's pleased he's here. "Don't get no ideas," I say, grabbing some joggers and pulling them on. I fasten the top few buttons of his shirt that I took when I left. "He's here about Dagger."

We step into the living room, and my stomach knots when I see Bully by the window, arms tense, eyes locked on something outside. Whizz is crouched beside him, setting up a strange-looking device, wires snaking across the table like nerves.

"What's going on?" I ask, the words sharp enough to bring Bully's attention to me.

"Whizz is checking for bugs," he says flatly.

"Dagger hasn't been here."

"To your knowledge," he mutters, eyes narrowing.

Beside me, Bria goes still. Her body tenses like she's bracing for an earthquake. "What did I miss?"

"I'll explain later," I whisper, but I'm not sure how I'll even begin.

Bully crosses his arms, muscles coiled. "Your sister deserves to know a psycho is stalking you."

Bria's head whips around, eyes wide and searching mine. I exhale slowly, my lungs tight. "I don't know for sure." But I do. Deep down, I do.

She gasps. "That's how he knows where you are all the time."

"I'm gonna scan the rooms," Whizz says. "And I need your mobile."

I hand it over, palms clammy. He plugs it into his laptop and starts moving through the room, scanning light fittings, behind frames, every crevice.

Bria disappears to get dressed, leaving me alone with Bully.

He gestures to a paper bag on the table. "Breakfast."

I blink. "Thanks." It's the first time he's brought me anything like that. When I peek inside and see two vanilla croissants, something in my chest squeezes. "I love these," I murmur.

His gaze flickers. "I know."

Whizz moves into the kitchen, and Bully sits down. "Sit with me," he says firmly, and I lower onto the couch. I pull off a piece of pastry, chewing slowly. I'm too on-edge to enjoy it. "I gave Whizz your old phone," he says. "There was an app installed. It was listening in to you."

I freeze. "What kind of app?"

"Something to monitor your mic. We think he put it there."

"But . . . he never had my phone," I say, heart pounding.

"Not that you knew of," he says cautiously. "But he could've come in here while you were asleep."

My blood runs cold. The croissant drops from my hand and back into the bag. My appetite vanishes. "Is that what you really think?" My voice cracks. He nods, just once. I gasp and cover my mouth, bile rising in my throat. "He was in my home?"

"It was installed a week before I got out of prison. That's how he knew."

"No. No, it's public. Anyone could've found that information out," I argue, but even I can hear the weakness in my voice.

"We kept it off the radar. Even my solicitor made sure no one knew."

A low groan escapes me. "He came into my house," I whisper. My voice barely exists. The tears I've been holding back burn at the corners of my eyes.

"I've spoken to security. They understand now. Dagger won't get in again."

I scoff bitterly. "Don't pretend that means anything. Not with him."

I glance up and see Bria in the doorway. Her ghostly expression tells me she heard every word. "We can go to the clubhouse, right?" she says. "It makes sense."

She's not wrong. Of course, it makes sense.

"No." My voice is firmer than I feel. "We have to stand on our own two feet."

"Bria's right," Bully says. "You'll be safer at the club until this is over."

I shoot to my feet. "And how exactly do you plan to end it?"

He rises too, his expression unreadable. "The details don't matter. It *will* be handled."

But his calm doesn't settle me. It terrifies me more.

CHAPTER SEVENTEEN

Bully

There's a steely glint in Liv's eye, and I know she's not gonna back down on this. I could force her, drag her to the club kicking and screaming. And I'd do that just to know she's safe. But something inside is begging me to do it differently this time. To listen to her and respect her decision. Our intense stare-off is interrupted when Whizz reappears, holding up a listening device.

"Fuck," I mutter.

"Fuck?" repeats Liv, glancing back and forth between us. "What is that?"

"It was a listening device," Whizz tells her. "I crushed it."

"Which is pointless if he's heard everything you've just said," snaps Bria, pacing nervously.

"He didn't," Whizz reassures her. "It was in one of Liv's handbags in her wardrobe. It wouldn't have picked us up in here." He sits beside his laptop and begins tapping away to check Liv's new phone.

"Explains how he knew things," mutters Liv. "I take that bag out with me. I also had it when you listed the things you knew about me," she says, glancing away.

Knowing she didn't tell him those personal things calms me some, and I offer a sympathetic smile. Proving to her I was right all along, that Dagger's been using her to get to me, doesn't make me feel better. The entire situation is shit.

"Your mobile isn't tracked," says Whizz. "Did you have that bag on you at The Woodthorpe?" Liv nods. "So, he didn't track you there. He either followed you or he heard your conversation." He closes the laptop and begins to pack his equipment away.

Liv suddenly looks alarmed. "Now what?"

I shrug. As hard as it is, I'm gonna do as she asked and give her space. "There's nothing else here. Whizz has checked everywhere. I've spoken to security, and they know not to let anyone past, especially not Dagger."

I head for the door, followed by Whizz, and when I glance back, she's watching me with her mouth hanging open in surprise. "Call me if you need anything," I say, opening the door. "I don't have your number, so don't expect me to call you." Her brows furrow. "And be careful, Liv."

We take the stairs, and once we step out through the back door, Whizz laughs. "Fuck, Pres, that was awkward."

"Tell me about it," I mutter, jumping on a shed roof and hauling myself up over the wall. I reach back to grab Whizz's equipment. "But it's what she wanted." We jump down into the next garden. "Did you add a tracker?" I ask.

Whizz smirks. "Of course. I've sent her number to your phone so you can track her." It's a shitty thing to do, but I have to make sure she's safe, and it's clear from her messages to that piece of shit that she's trying to handle all this in her own way.

We pull up around the back of the club—an agreement we made to be less in the firing line should the Scorpions try to take a shot—when my mobile beeps.

I smile when I see the number, immediately saving it under 'Liv'.

> **Liv: My number. Just in case you want it.**

> **Me: Thank you. I hope you're okay. It was a lot to take in.**

> **Liv: Bria's freaking out. Nothing new there.**

I head inside, not checking again until I'm in my office. I'm surprised to find another message.

> **Liv: There's nothing between me and Dagger, Liam. I swear x**

I stare at the message for a minute, my emotions mixing up a storm. I take a breath before replying.

> **Me: It's your life, Liv, but please, don't date a biker.**

I won't handle any guy being with her. I know that. She knows that. But somehow, a biker hits so much worse.

> **Liv: Dating is the last thing on my mind. X**

I sit back in my chair before typing out my next words.

> **Me: I've made so many mistakes, Liv. Hurting you was my biggest. You never deserved that, and I know you don't believe**

it, but I love you. I will always love you. For what it's worth, I'm sorry x

I stare, holding my breath, waiting for her to reply. It doesn't come. A minute passes, then two. I throw my phone in the drawer. I have a war to finish, and waiting for Liv to respond is just tying me up in knots.

Church is chaos. The men are all trying to talk at once, all wanting to be heard. As I enter, silence falls. Misty is waiting in my chair, and she stands, wagging. Now Liv's gone, I might have to face it that Misty is gonna be the only female in my life. I smirk at that thought.

She jumps down, making room for me, and once I sit, she jumps in my lap.

"Whizz filled us in," says Taz.

I nod. "Good. Smiler, over to you."

Smiler clears his throat. "I sat down with Ragnar, Boss, and Stretch to work out a plan. It ain't gonna be easy. I've been watching Dagger's men, and they're clever. Too clever. They don't ride the same formations, they don't even ride the same routes, and they hardly ever ride with Dagger. It's like they don't want to draw attention to themselves, yet they don't want to hide away. And Dagger is like a fucking ghost lately."

"Taking them on the road is near impossible," Ragnar cuts in. "I know you wanted it that way, Pres, but hitting them at base makes more sense."

I shake my head. "We tried that. It didn't work."

Whizz grins, turning his laptop my way. "What if we attend a party?"

I peer closer at the poster on screen. "Where'd yah get that?"

"One of his men emailed it to Dagger, and I'm monitoring his emails," he says with a wink.

I grin, turning it to Smiler. "Would this work?"

He half shrugs. "I mean, it's tight," he says, checking his watch. "But if we wait 'til dark, get in towards the end when their guard is down."

I nod, banging the gavel on the table. "We'll meet back here at nine for instructions."

The men head out, but Taz lingers back. "You reckon that party is for Lila?"

"That's what the poster said, *in remembrance*."

He shakes his head. "It don't feel right, Pres. Why celebrate her life when he was the one who brought her down?"

"I don't know, Taz. All I do know is that I'm sick of waiting. I want the piece of shit dead before sunrise."

Olivia

I managed to convince Bria into seeing our friends tonight. I needed some space, and her worrying was driving me insane. The second she left, I jumped into the bath for a nice, long soak. Then I put on my fluffy pyjamas and sank into the couch to watch a movie.

But even as Tom Hardy demands my attention, my mobile taunts me. I pick it up for the hundredth time to read Bully's message. His words seem genuine, and I don't remember the last time he ever wrote me a text like this. An apology.

My finger hovers over the reply button, just like it has done more than ten times at least. It would be easy to forgive him, and lord knows

I want to. But we've been here too many times. The first was when we'd only been together a few months. He slept with a club whore and immediately confessed because the guilt ate him alive. The second time was a random woman on a night out, but then we'd been together a year. So, when he went inside, I relaxed. He couldn't cheat in prison. Or so I thought. And knowing about it is bad enough, but watching it, hearing her say those words, *I love you*, is too much.

> **Me: Why did you do it to me again?**

Its' seconds before his reply comes, and my heart is beating in my throat as I open it.

> **Bully: Because I'm an idiot. It was sex, Liv. Just sex.**

> **Me: Did you have feelings for her? Be honest, I can take it.**

> **Bully: No. But I think she felt things for me. I brushed it off. I just wanted sex. Being inside, away from you, was too hard and she was a distraction. I didn't even give her a second thought after she got fired.**

> **Me: You've really hurt me.**

> **Bully: And I hate myself for it. What are you doing?**

> **Me: Watching a movie.**

> **Bully: Bet it's got Tom Hardy in it.**

I smile to myself.

Me: Of course.

Bully: Is Bria okay now?

Me: I forced her to go out with the girls and give me some peace.

His reply takes a little longer to come.

Bully: Liv, you shouldn't be alone.

I roll my eyes and put my phone back on the table. I'm not in the mood for his alpha bullshit right now.

Ten minutes later, there's a knock at the door.

My heart jumps. Of course, he couldn't stay away. I bite back a smile as I cross the room, half-annoyed, half-relieved, and pull the door open with a shake of my head.

"I'm fi—" The word dies on my lips. It's not Bully. It's *Dagger*.

My stomach drops clean through the floor. I blink, frozen for a beat too long before instinct kicks in. I step back and pull the door halfway shut, leaving just enough space to poke my head through.

"Hi," I say, but the word comes out stiff, brittle. My throat is dry. I can barely swallow.

He tilts his head, a smirk tugging at his mouth. "You expecting someone else?"

"Yeah," I say, trying to keep my voice steady. "Bully's on his way."

He doesn't flinch. Doesn't blink. Just smiles wider, like we're sharing some private joke I don't understand. "Thought I'd check on you."

"You really don't have to." I grip the edge of the door tighter, my knuckles aching. "I'm fine."

"I was just passing," he says, as casual as if we were old friends bumping into each other on the street.

I force a laugh. "How'd you get past security? They usually call up first."

He shrugs like it's no big deal. "Must've been my lucky day." My pulse hammers in my ears. The air feels too hot, too tight. "You gonna invite me in?" he asks, voice light but eyes sharp.

I shake my head. "It's not really a good time with Bully on his way and all."

That's when his smile changes to cruel. His hand slams against the door. Hard. I flinch and let go on instinct, and the door flies open. Dagger steps inside without hesitation, shutting it behind him with a quiet click that makes every hair on my body stand on end.

"Bully's not coming, mama," he says, voice low and satisfied.

My back hits the wall. "What do you want?" I ask, barely above a whisper. My fingers twitch at my sides, useless. My phone's still on the table, meters away. Too far. He takes a slow look around, his eyes scanning the space like he owns it.

"I wanted to see how you're settling in. Place is nicer than I expected." His eyes land on me again. "Too nice for someone who doesn't know how to lock a door properly."

"I do lock it."

He grins. "Not well enough."

A sick feeling rolls through me. My skin goes cold. "You've been here before," I say, the words trembling out of me. "Haven't you?" He doesn't deny it. My hands curl into fists. "You bugged my phone."

He shrugs again, as if it's all a game. "It's amazing what people give away when they think they're alone."

"You listened to me," I say, the horror sinking in. "You've *been* listening."

"Don't act so surprised. You should've seen this coming." His voice dips, low and warning.

I shake my head. "You're angry because of your wife, and I get that."

For the first time, his smile fades. His eyes go dead. "I warned you," he says, his voice calm and terrifying, "but you picked the wrong side, Liv."

I'm already shaking my head frantically. "I didn't. I haven't. I want to stay out of it."

"So you keep saying," he mutters, picking up my mobile. "But then he gives you a sob story and you believe it. You forgive him. And he doesn't deserve it. He doesn't deserve you."

A chill ripples through me. I glance towards the hallway, trying to judge if I can make a run for it. He sees it. "Don't," he warns. "Let's not make this ugly."

I clench my jaw then take a calming breath. "You loved her," I whisper, fighting the tears in my eyes. "Like I love him."

His eyes snap to mine. "Don't compare what I had with Lila to you and him," he sneers angrily. "Because of him, I had to ruin the one thing I loved."

For a second, we just stare at each other. My heartbeat is in my throat. I'm afraid if I breathe too loudly, he'll pounce. "How did you find out about them?"

"She told me," he says coldly, flicking through my phone. "After she found out she was pregnant." A gasp escapes me, and I slam my hand over my mouth. He glances up, smirking. "You didn't know that little piece of information?" I shake my head. "I can't have kids," he says, like it's just a fact. "So, I did some digging. Wasn't hard once I knew where to look. And when I told her the baby couldn't be mine . . ." He trails off, a sick sort of satisfaction curling around his words. "She told me everything." I go still. My legs feel like they'll give out. "Tying her up helped," he adds with a twisted little laugh. "Torturing her . . .

yeah, that really got her talking. Once she started, she couldn't stop. I think," he tilts his head, almost thoughtful, "I think she was relieved."

"Then she killed herself?"

He grins wider, almost laughing. "She didn't have the balls." He shakes his head like he's lost in the memory. "I had her fired, made sure they had all the details to open the investigation. I even let my guys rail her like a fucking train, and still, she wouldn't end it. She wanted the trial to go ahead because she knew Bully wouldn't talk. It was her chance to lie her way out of it."

I frown. "But you had the video evidence."

"That was gonna be my big reveal," he says, amused. "But then, she started getting crazy, threatening to call the police, to tell them she was 'raped' by my guys." The way he says the word, like it isn't true, makes me sick to my stomach, but I bite back my tears. "I had no choice. To make it believable, it had to end before the trial. I couldn't risk her being let off, cos then she would have had no reason to end her life."

My frown deepens. "You killed her?" He's deranged. His whole demeanor is off, like he's finally over the edge.

His evil smile confirms it. "She couldn't stay in this world without me." He sighs heavily. "Now, you've got a choice, mama," he says, voice low and coiled with threat. "And let's be crystal clear." He places my phone on the table with a soft, deliberate *click*. Then he steps in, too close, stealing the air from the room. "You need to pick a side."

My throat is so tight, I can barely swallow. "What if I don't want to pick?"

He smirks, like he's been hoping I'd say that. "Then I'll pick for you."

I flinch as his hand lifts, not in a strike but something worse. His finger brushes slowly across my collarbone, and I recoil, closing my eyes in revulsion as he trails it over the swell of my breast.

"First things first," he murmurs, tapping the ink that marks me—Bully's name etched just above my heart. "We've got to get rid of *this*."

I raise my hands to shove him back, panic choking me, but he grabs my wrists and pins them to my sides like it's nothing. Then, before I can twist away, I feel his breath on my skin and then teeth.

He *bites* down, hard, right over the tattoo.

Pain sears through me. I gasp, a cry rising in my throat, but he shoves his fingers into my mouth before I can make a sound. I gag, choking, every muscle locking in fear. Tears stream down my cheeks.

When he pulls back, he's grinning. My blood is smeared across his mouth. He licks it, and my stomach churns. My body goes rigid, heart hammering so violently, I think it might crack a rib. "Better," he sneers. "I'll clean up, then we can make it official." I stare blankly, not daring to move as his eyes assess my body. "You've no idea how many times I've jerked off to you in the shower." He laughs. "Mama, I'm gonna fuck you raw."

I fight the urge to vomit as he turns away to reach for a towel. Casual, like this is just another day for him. My eyes flick down to the counter, where the towel had been, and there's a knife. *A sharp one.*

My breath catches. Every nerve in my body screams not to move, but I ignore them. Slowly, carefully, I slide my hand across the counter. Inch by inch. His back is still to me as my fingers brush the handle until I grip it tight.

My pulse is roaring in my ears now, everything else falling away—his muttering, the towel, even the sickness.

He starts to turn and his eyes widen. I *lunge*. The blade sinks deep, right into his eye. He screams. A raw, animal sound that rips through the apartment. His hands fly up, but I'm already backing away. The knife still in his face, blood gushes between his fingers as he collapses to his knees, howling in agony.

The front door slams open behind me. "Liv!"

But I'm already falling, sliding down the wall, shaking violently.

I don't know if I'm going to throw up or pass out, but for the first time in what feels like hours, I can *breathe*.

CHAPTER EIGHTEEN

Bully

The roar of bike engines slices through the night like a battle cry.

We ride in formation, tight, controlled, lethal. Boss leads up front, rigid like stone, his patch gleaming under the moonlight. I ride just behind him, black hoodie pulled up beneath my kutte, jaw clenched, fists tight around the grips. Behind me, Taz, Ragnar, Brains, and Smiler ride staggered, the weight of war heavy across their shoulders.

Stretch is tail gunner, riding anchor with a sawn-off slung across his chest. Eyes on mirrors, always watching our six. And somewhere trailing behind is Tally in the van, carrying everything we'll need to end this tonight.

Nobody talks.

The only sound is the deep, unified thunder of Harley engines tearing across the asphalt. We're ghosts in the dark, *death on wheels*.

As the bar comes into view, a flicker of yellow neon buzzing weakly against the gloom, Boss raises his fist. Every rider knows what that means—slow down, get ready.

We don't brake gently. We don't roll in unannounced. They need to hear us and know they're about to die. We kill the engines, a collective screech of tyres eating the gravel as we line up outside. One after the other, we dismount, our boots hitting the road heavy. Tally swings the van door open and begins throwing out weapons. I grab the M249. This belt-fed monster doesn't politely knock—it rips the door off the fucking hinges.

The music inside stops, and it brings a smile to my lips. They've heard us. "Light it up," I order.

Then, hell breaks loose.

I squeeze the trigger, unleashing fury. The front wall of the bar explodes in splinters and screams as bullets punch through timber and bodies alike. Windows shatter and bottles burst, cascading down the walls mixed with blood.

We move forward, giving no room for them to come back at us. And once we're inside, Dagger's remaining men scramble around, some ducking behind tables but most don't even get that far.

Brains and Taz move in beside me, each armed with ARs, mowing down anything that breathes and doesn't wear a Bastards patch. Ragnar kicks in the side door, tossing in a stun grenade. The boom shakes the floorboards, and the strobe of light blinds anyone left standing.Boss moves in clean and brutal, shotgun in one hand, axe in the other. Smiler, grinning like his namesake, follows, picking off stragglers with deadly precision, never missing a shot. The floor's already slick with blood and glass. Bodies are left twitching, moaning, and gurgling.

Stretch and Tally guard the perimeter. Any poor bastard thinking of running will get dropped before he makes it to the road.

When I'm certain everything is still, I hold up my hand and the gunfire stops. My ears ring with it as I scan the room for any movement. "Start turning over bodies," I order. "I need to see him for myself." And as my men move around, doing as I've asked, I pull out my mobile and check on Liv's location, just in case she's decided to sneak out and join her sister. When I see she's still at home, I relax, tucking it way again.

"Pres," calls Taz, "he ain't here."

I frown. "What?"

"There's no sign of Dagger. We've checked every man. There are eighteen bodies. That leaves Dagger unaccounted for."

Anger pulsates through me. "Why wouldn't he fucking be here? Lila was his old lady."

Boss slaps me on the back. "I know you want him, Pres, but without his club, he's nothing. It's only a matter of time before we catch up with him."

"We need to get Liv to the club," I snap. "Once he knows about this, she'll be his target."

"You want me to send the prospects to get her?" asks Taz.

I laugh. "Nah, she'll give them hell. I'm gonna have to throw her over my shoulder for this one." I hand my gun to Boss. "Burn this place to the ground. The police aren't responding 'til smoke goes up, so the second you light it, get the hell out of here."

Olivia

"Liv," Bria calls, shaking me, "answer me."

My eyes find hers, swollen red from crying. I have no tears. They're all gone. She glances at my chest. "You're bleeding," she whispers, and suddenly, pain burns the spot, like her seeing it is a reminder that it hurts. "We need to call the club."

I slide my eyes to where Dagger is lying on his back, the knife sticking out from his eye like it's mocking me. A sob escapes me, and I slap a hand over my mouth. "Is he dead?" I whisper, my voice strained. She nods, slow and careful, like she's terrified of my reaction. "He was going to . . ." I sob harder. "I had no choice."

She grips the tops of my arms, nodding. "It's okay. I believe you. Bully can make this go away."

I shake my head. "No. I have to call the police. When I tell them what happened, they'll understand. It was self-defence."

"Listen to me, Liv," she says sternly, and I wait for her words. "You're going to do what I say now, okay?" I nod. "Go and shower. I'm going to call Bully. Let's get this mess cleared up." I've never seen her so calm, so I find myself pushing to stand. She places herself between me and Dagger, like I haven't already got his image burned into my brain. I shudder.

I stay under the hot spray of the shower until the bathroom is filled with steam, making it hard to see my hand in front of my face. It's only when the door opens and Bully appears that I burst into tears. He throws his kutte over the sink then steps under the spray, wrapping his arms around me as I cry against his chest.

I don't know how long we stand there, but my tears have dried and I'm exhausted. Bully turns the shower off and grabs a fluffy towel, all while still holding me to him, like he's afraid I'll fall if he lets go. Maybe I will.

He wraps me tightly then begins to fight out of his wet jeans and shirt, wrapping a towel around his waist. No words are spoken as he scoops me into his arms and carries me from the bathroom straight into the bedroom. He sits me on the edge of the bed and grabs another towel. Standing beside me, he gently rubs my hair.

"Liv," he whispers, and I startle at his voice. "You're safe now." I exhale, like his words have the ability to make that statement true. And suddenly, I feel lighter. My shoulders slump, and Bully places a gentle kiss on my head. "I'm sorry."

His apology hangs between us as he takes the hairdryer, aiming it at my wet locks. He runs his fingers through the strands, and I close my eyes, picturing all the times I've felt close to him. Yet this is the first he's shown me any kind of tenderness.

I zone out, blinking when the dryer turns off and Bully runs a brush through my hair. He begins to plait it, and I frown in confusion. "Are you plaiting my hair?" I whisper. After everything that's happened in the last few hours, it's strange that this sticks out the most.

"I did a few sessions when I was inside."

A laugh escapes me, sounding foreign amongst the heaviness. "Sessions on hair?" I turn, glancing at him over my shoulder.

He shrugs. "One day I might need this shit."

"Like?"

He inhales deeply. "If I ever have a daughter." My breath catches. It's not the answer I expected.

Bully stands, going to my drawer and digging around for some fresh pyjamas. He brings a short and vest set over. "It's boring in there, so you find yourself going to anything just to break the day up." He gathers the top in his hands, scrunching it and holding it above my head. I raise my arms, and he gently tugs it over me, waiting for it to cover my chest before removing the towel. His eyes land on the bite mark again, but just like in the shower, he doesn't ask. The towel remains around my waist, so he crouches before me, holding the shorts there while I step into them. He's being so attentive, I want to cry.

"I heard all the guys talking about a course on parenting. I had nothing better to do, so I went along. We had to read stories," he smiles at the memory. "My personal favourite is *The Gruffalo*, in case you wondered," he says, pulling the sheets back on the bed. He pats the mattress, and I climb in. "That clever little bastard mouse is a hero. The next week, we learned about hair. I can now confidently secure a ponytail and a plait," he tells me. "I know that speaking to the bump pre-birth is important for bonding between baby and dad. I even know how to change a nappy." He pulls the sheets over me. "Turns out, it was a good course." He takes his shirt that I wore last night for bed, and pulls it on, then he pulls his boxers back on, the only thing that somehow managed to stay dry. "Sleep now, Liv."

I grab his hand, and he stops. "I can't be on my own," I whisper.

His eyes fill with pain, then he places a kiss to the back of my hand before placing it beside me on the bed. "I'll be right outside. I'm not going anywhere."

Bully

I slip out the room, closing the door and resting against it. My heart aches for Liv. So much has happened in the last few weeks, so much I wanted to protect her from.

Bria appears in my line of sight, so I move off from the door and head into the living room. "Don't say it," I warn.

"It's nothing you don't already know," she spits. "If you'd forced her to the clubhouse, this would never have happened."

"No one could've predicted this shitshow," I hiss, closing the gap between us. I'm angry, lashing out even though she doesn't deserve it. "If I'd dragged her to the club, she would've hated me more."

"He could've killed her."

I scrub my hands over my face. "I know," I say, my voice barely a whisper.

Taz joins us, removing his gloves. "It's like new in there," he tells us proudly. "Fuck, it's been a while since I had to sort shit myself."

"Those men who came," says Bria, glancing between us, "who were they? Will they tell anyone?"

I shake my head. "They work for the club doing cleanup," I tell her. "Dagger will be buried tonight where no one can find him."

"That's not enough," she snaps. "How do I know this won't come back on Liv?"

I clench my jaw. "Do you think I'd let that happen?" I growl. "She's my old lady. I wouldn't let it touch her."

"It already did."

Taz sighs. "It's done now. There's no point bitching about it."

"She wanted to call the police, hand herself in," she mutters, turning away and heading for the window. "She said they'd understand it was self-defence." She peers out, staring down at the ground below. "I can't lose her, Bully."

I move behind her, wrapping my arms around her shoulders. She sags against me. "You won't. I'd never let her go down for this. I should've protected her better, done more . . ." I trail off, hating how right I am.

"Bully!"

We both startle at the sound of Liv's painful cry, and I rush to her room, bursting in to find her tangled in the sheets, her body twisting from side to side as she cries out for me. I dive onto the bed, cupping her face. "I'm here, Liv. I'm right here," I say, my voice full of panic as she settles, and I realise she's so deep in sleep, she's lost. She sobs, her body vibrating. I slide in beside her, glancing at Bria, who's standing in the doorway silently crying. Liv immediately curls into me, her head resting against my chest, her nose pressed to my throat. I wrap her in my arms, our legs tangling the way they always do when we're together.

"Stay with her," Bria whispers. "I'll come and get you if you're needed."

I wake with a start, and it disturbs Liv, who also wakes. Her eyes find mine, and she smiles. It's cute and sleepy, but I see the second everything comes flooding back because she gasps like a physical pain has hit her, and her smile fades. "I thought it was a nightmare," she whispers, her voice heavy from sleep.

I place a kiss on her forehead. "It was, Liv. Just a bad dream."

"He was going to take me. Make me his."

Each word punches me in the chest. "I'm sorry I left you. I should've stayed."

Her brows furrow as she's hit with memories. "He said I had to choose a side or he'd choose for me."

I rest my chin on her head, holding her against my chest as I stroke lazy circles on her back. "He can't hurt you anymore."

She frowns, like the next words are hard. "Lila was pregnant."

I swallow the shock. "He told you that?" She nods. "He could have been lying, Liv. We won't ever know the truth."

"I don't think he was lying. He told me too many details, personal details. She was pregnant, Bully, and it was yours."

I cup her cheek as she brings her eyes to mine, "We don't know that for sure. She could have been fucking other guys in there."

"Don't do that," she mutters, disappointment pouring from her. "Don't put the blame on her, she told you she loved you. She wasn't fucking around. And she was pregnant with your child. Doesn't that bother you?"

I look away, gathering my words carefully. "I don't know what you want me to do with that information, Liv. She's not here anymore. My focus is on you now, not her, not some kid I knew nothing about."

She settles back against my chest, and we fall into silence before she asks, "Will I go to prison?"

I pull back again, surprised, running my eyes over her innocent face. "No, Liv. You're not going anywhere."

"I have to tell them," she says, her face full of concern.

"Liv, you can't go to the police."

"But when I tell them . . . when I say what he did . . ."

"Liv, it's not an option. Too much would come up, so many things that you'd be dragged into."

She blinks. "Club things." I nod. "But I don't know anything about that stuff."

"They'd think you're lying to cover for me."

"What about him . . . his b-body?"

"Gone."

She pushes to sit, now looking concerned. "Gone where?"

"We took care of it."

She shakes her head, throwing the sheets back and swinging her legs over the edge. "Liv," I whisper, my voice pleading as she races to the door, ripping it open. "Fuck's sake," I mutter to myself as I dive up to follow.

She rounds the kitchen, skidding to a stop and staring at the spot where Dagger was laid out hours ago. "You have to bring him back," she cries desperately, "or they'll think I covered it up."

"No one will find him."

"They will. People will ask where he is, and I can't lie, Bully. I can't lie to the police." Her eyes are wide, darting around in panic, and her complexion is pale.

"You have to calm down," I say firmly, grabbing her upper arms, trying to look her in the eye. "It's going to be okay."

"I killed him," she yells frantically, "and I have to report it."

Bria marches in, taking Liv from me and slapping her hard across the face. Liv gasps, and rage fills me. She might be her sister, but that doesn't mean she gets to lay a hand on her. Liv immediately begins to cry, and Bria nods. "It's good to cry," she tells her. "Let it out. But you are not going to the police."

"Bria," I mutter, "she's delicate."

"She's in shock," she snaps, "and she needs hard truths."

I watch helplessly as she fixes Liv with a glare. "Dagger is gone. It's done. We don't need to get into a state over him, Liv. He deserved it. It was him or you." Liv nods slowly, her tears dripping from her cheeks. "So, listen to Bully. He's going to help you."

She finally looks to me, her eyes searching for answers. "We were together," I say as Bria steps back, leaving me to take over and fill her in on an alibi. *Not that she'll need it.* Taking the Scorpions off our streets was a good result all round, and the police won't be spending too much time trying to find answers. "All night, from when I came over yesterday." She nods. "Just us, because Bria was with friends at the bar. We watched movies."

"With Tom Hardy," she mutters.

I smile, also nodding. "Yeah, a Tom marathon. Then Bria came home with Taz. We all went to bed." She nods again. "But it won't come to this because there's no real connection between you and Dagger."

CHAPTER NINETEEN

Olivia

I stare out the window as grey clouds roll in, dark and low. The sky feels heavy, swallowing what little light remains as rain begins to fall. It taps the glass like a gentle lullaby, soothing me in a way nothing else does right now. Maybe it mirrors something deeper inside me, that stillness, that ache. The one I haven't been able to shift for the last few days.

Not since . . . *Dagger*.

His lifeless image assaults my brain, just like it does over and over. Uninvited. Unwanted.

I feel Bully step into the room, his eyes burning into me, watching me. He's watched me a lot these last few days, closer than usual, perhaps expecting me to break. I haven't. *Not yet.* But I feel like my mind is pushing me to, wanting that peace that I helped Dagger to reach. I shudder. The intrusive thoughts are loud, too loud to ignore some days.

I inhale deep and turn to face him, forcing a smile. "Everything okay?"

He nods, his eyes still checking me over warily. "Are you okay?"

I drop my feet to the floor and stand, tired of hearing the same question. Can someone be okay when they've murdered another? "I need some air," I tell him, heading for the door.

"Liv, it's raining," he calls after me, like I haven't just spent the last hour staring out the window.

The security guard looks up from his newspaper as I step out the lift. It's a new guy, and I suspect that's down to Bully. The door to the stairs springs open, and Bully appears, out of breath. He holds up a jacket for me, and I roll my eyes, going out into the rain without taking it. He follows, dumping the jacket on the security guy's desk.

Whenever I step out these doors, it's with Bully tailing me. He doesn't speak to me, doesn't even fall into step with me . . . he just follows. I turn to face him, walking backwards. "I don't need you following me." He remains silent. "I'm perfectly capable of walking alone." When he still doesn't respond, I growl in frustration and spin back around, tipping my head back and holding my arms out, allowing the rain to soak me.

The street is busy with people rushing home from work, trying to avoid getting too wet as they dodge around one another. I walk slow, earning myself a few huffs as they dart past me, eyeing me with irritation. I smile. They don't know how lucky they are.

I close my eyes, slowing to a stop. I jolt forward, and my eyes shoot open, squealing in surprise as Bully catches me right before I hit the ground. A man mutters a few choice words as he speeds around us. "Fuck you," Bully calls after him. "Are you okay?" he asks, and I nod, our eyes locked in some kind of war.

I'm still hurting. Still haunted by the images of him with Lila. Still hearing the words 'I love you' play on repeat. But I can't deny the heat crackling between us as he holds me against him.

Each night since Dagger, he's held me until I've fallen asleep then crept from my room, only having to return after each nightmare.

"Why don't you ever spend the night?" I whisper, blinking as rain drips from my brows. "You leave but then have to keep coming back when I wake."

He brushes a strand of hair that clings to my cheek. "I don't deserve to spend the night, Liv."

I inhale sharply, my heart aching. And then I kiss him, slow, gentle. As I slide my hands over his cheeks and into his hair, it's hungry and desperate. A need for connection. A need to feel.

Bully's hands cling to my waist as he walks me out of the crowd without breaking the kiss. My back hits a wall, and I realise we're in an alleyway. Bully pulls back, keeping eye contact. His breathing is laboured, and I see the lust burning like embers. "I love you," he whispers, his expression changing to sympathy, "but you're not ready for this." His words sting, and my hands immediately drop to my sides. He's rejecting me. *Rejecting me.* As if he feels the sudden tension, he cups my face, trying to force me to look him in the eye. *I don't.* "Liv, you're spiralling. If we did this, you'd regret it. I know you."

I scoff, feeling the rage burning in my chest. "You don't know me," I spit, shaking his hands from me. He steps back. "If you did, you'd stop watching me like I'm a fucking China doll." I push against his chest, but he doesn't budge. "I'm not going to break, Bully."

"And this is you, is it?" he asks. "Fucking in an alleyway like a desperate bitch in heat?" I slap him. It's hard, instantly stinging my palm, and the sound echoes off the walls as silence spreads between us. He's shocked as he grips his cheek, bringing his eyes to me.

"I forgot you like fucking in secret, Bully. Behind closed doors. Behind people's backs."

He grazes his lower lip between his teeth, his eyes burning into mine while he gets control of his anger. "It's in the past," he eventually says, dropping his hand from his face. The bright red handprint makes me feel guilty, and I look away. "I'm not that man anymore." He takes a few steps back. "Now, are you walking or not?"

Things feel strained. Maybe there are words we haven't said, things we both resent and things we can't forgive.

Bully followed me around the entire park, a good thirty-minute walk. All from a distance. Not just a few steps back like normal, but a good twenty feet.

And now, he's in the kitchen, laughing and joking with Bria, like everything is fine. But it's not, because whenever I step into the room, he goes quiet. He avoids my eyes. *And I hate it.*

I'm the one who should be mad still. *He hurt me.* He has no right to act like the wounded party here. And as laughter rings out, it sinks me deeper into a mood.

Another half-hour passes before Bria passes with a bowl of whatever he's cooked. She offers a smile. "You okay?" I nod, just like I always do when she asks. "I'm gonna eat this in my room," she adds, disappearing.

Bully appears in the doorway. "I know you're not eating much right now," he begins, and my eyes find the faint mark my hand left on his cheek, "but I worked hard. Come," he orders, holding out a hand.

I reluctantly go into the kitchen, not taking his hand. He sighs heavily, following me.

I stop at the table, which is laid beautifully. Bully pulls out my seat, and I lower into it. "I thought we could change your favourite flowers," he says, pointing to the spray of pink baby's breath in the centre. "I asked the florist, and these are popular." I remain silent as he takes a seat opposite me. "I learned how to cook," he adds, pointing to the lamb sliced thinly on a serving plate. He lifts a lid on a dish to reveal buttery potatoes and vegetables. "Will you try to eat something . . . for me?" I give a slight nod, and he smiles in relief.

He begins to serve the meat. "I haven't told the guys I can cook," he says, almost smiling. "But I might surprise them with a home-cooked curry soon. It'll blow Birdy's steak pie out the window."

He loads my plate with vegetables before settling back in his chair and nodding at me, pushing me to try his food. I carefully pick up my fork and stab it in the meat. I shudder when I picture Dagger again, unable to lift the fork any farther. Bully's movement grabs my attention as he drags his chair around the table next to me. He takes the fork from my hand and picks up the knife. I watch as he cuts a piece then adds a potato to the fork before carefully bringing it to my lips, waiting patiently until I open up.

I close my eyes as the meat practically melts in my mouth. I haven't eaten in days, unless you count the dry crackers Bria force-fed me. My stomach growls in appreciation, and Bully smiles, loading up the next forkful.

Bully

Each mouthful feels like a small victory, and when she's halfway through, she shakes her head. She's eaten more than I thought she would, and I remain beside her as I finish my own.

I clear the plates then go to the fridge and retrieve the lemon cheesecake. "You've always been a dessert kind of girl," I tell her as I place it on the table. I think I almost see a smile as I take a seat. "And I know how you love lemon gin, so I created a lemon gin cheesecake. I don't know if that's a thing, but I figured drinking wouldn't lead anywhere good, so adding it to a dessert would be the better option."

I scoop some onto a spoon, raising it to her lips. As she licks it from the spoon, I have to divert my eyes elsewhere. It's like a slow torture watching her eat when all I want to do is kiss her perfect lips.

"I'm sorry," she eventually whispers, and our eyes meet. "For earlier. For hitting you."

I force a smile. It was a shock. Liv has never reacted like that towards me. Her lashing out is just another thing concerning me, like her silence, and like the distant look in her eye whenever I try to reach her.

"Don't apologise, Liv. It's the least I deserve for everything I've put you through," I reply, using my thumb to wipe away some of the cream from the corner of her mouth. I lick it clean.

"I left a mark," she whispers sadly, raising her hand to my face and cupping the cheek she hit.

I glance up and find tears in her eyes. I drop the spoon and turn to face her. "It's fine. I've had worse," I say, laughing to reassure her. "Any mark on my skin from you is one hundred percent wanted."

"I don't want to live here anymore," she announces, her voice barely a whisper. Her eyes glance to the corner where Dagger had been. "I feel like he's here. Watching me. Haunting me."

I hadn't even thought about that, and I mentally kick myself. "Shit, Liv. Sorry, I didn't think. I'll find you a new place," I say, pushing to stand as I grab my mobile from my pocket.

"No," she says quickly, grabbing my hand, and I pause. "Can I come and stay at the club?"

It's not what I was expecting, and I lower into my seat again. "Of course. You know that place is your home too."

She nods, relief passing over her face. I pull her against me and kiss the top of her head. "Go and pack what you need. I'll send the guys to clear the place later and put it all in storage."

"Thank you," she whispers.

We arrive at the clubhouse, and I instantly relax. Staying with Liv was my priority, but, fuck, I missed this place. The prospects take her bags and look to me for direction. I don't want to read too much into this. For all I know, it could be temporary until she feels able to get another place. "Have the room on my floor made up," I direct. I want to keep my eye on her, especially with her recurring nightmares, so having her on a different floor wouldn't work. But keeping her out of my bed, *our bed*, makes things less messy.

Bria follows them. "I'll grab a spare room on any floor," she calls back over her shoulder.

Taz pops his head out the office door. "We got church in two, Pres," he reminds me. Another thing I've missed.

I feel Liv's hand slip into mine. It's gentle, barely there, but as our fingers interlace, I realise she's not ready to be apart. So, I keep hold of her hand and lead her towards the room where some of the brothers have already settled down. Misty barks in greeting, jumping down from my chair and wagging her tail as she sniffs around my feet. I tickle her behind the ear, still keeping hold of Liv's hand. I scoop Misty up and sit on my chair, pulling Liv into my lap and passing Misty to her. The brothers watch through curious eyes. A non-patched member has never been in this room, especially during church and especially not an old lady.

Taz enters, frowning slightly when he spots us, but choosing wisely to remain quiet as he closes the door and sits.

"I know this is . . . unusual," I begin, "but I need updating on the Scorpions and, unfortunately, that involves Liv too." Maybe hearing everything might help her to heal.

Taz gives a shrug before standing. "Okay. I spoke to the chief of police. The cops are done with it. They're calling it a robbery gone sideways, like maybe some rival crew tried to hit them and things got messy. No one's digging further. Far as they're concerned, it's over."

"And what about Dagger?" I ask, feeling Liv tense. She needs to hear this. She needs to know she's not gonna be pulled up, that this won't come back on her.

"It was a mission," says Smiler, grinning over at Taz.

"But we managed to get him a few feet away from the site. He was found the next day, and they just assumed he'd somehow got away and was chased down and killed. It's good having people on the inside," says Taz.

"So, the investigation is being wrapped up," I confirm.

"Pretty much," says Taz. "Either way, it's not coming back on us."

I nod with satisfaction, gently squeezing Liv's thigh. "You wanna go find Bria?" I ask her. She nods, keeping hold of Misty and heading out.

I wait for the door to close again before exhaling heavily. "Now, tell me everything."

"Not as clean-cut as that," says Taz. "A few questions were raised, including how they missed Dagger's body on the first sweep. Our man on the inside deflected, mentioned the lighting being a problem. Our name was raised as possible suspects, but the chief shut that down. Said he'd personally seen a few of the guys on a ride out at the exact time. It's all tied up in a pretty little bow. The chief said himself,

Scorpions were poison. Every week, something new—stabbings, girls gone missing, dealers popping up like weeds. Now? Quiet. Streets are breathing again."

"He did tell us we gotta lay low for a while. Maybe step up on charity work, and keep our noses clean until this shitstorm dies a death," adds Smiler.

I relax back in my chair. "Without the Scorpions hanging over us, that shouldn't be an issue." I turn to Boss. "Plan another ride-out. Find a kid who's being bullied or some shit. We'll do an escort run or even a damn prom. We need the community on side again." Then, I take my attention to Tally. "How are the figures looking?"

He nods. "Pretty damn good, Pres, considering. Things are starting to look up since those fuckers got put down."

"That's good news," I mutter. "Anything else I should know?"

Taz shakes his head. "Go and look after your old lady," he says. "We got everything under control."

"Right now, she ain't my old lady," I say, suddenly feeling exhausted. "I don't know if I'll ever get her back."

"She's here, isn't she," says Mad Dog. "That tells you all you need to know."

I push to stand. "Let's hope you're right, brother."

CHAPTER TWENTY

Olivia

I've been in and out of this club for years. I know its rhythm like muscle memory—the way the floor creaks near the back stairs, the whir of the old beer fridge behind the bar, the late-night laughs that drift in through the bedroom windows from the guys staying up late to work on their bikes.

But this time, everything feels different. Hollow.

I walk into the main room in one of Bully's oversized shirts and a pair of shorts. The place is busy, with guys at the bar, music on low, and a few brothers playing pool. Yet the second I enter, I feel a shift in mood.

No one looks my way. Not like before. There are a few half-glances, quick nods like reflexes, but there's no banter. No 'hey Liv' from Taz. No sarcastic 'you lost, princess?' from Boss. It's like I'm invisible. Like I'm radioactive and everyone knows but me.

I spot Stretch behind the bar and head over. He's one of the more reserved bikers, someone I can usually chat to without all the banter. He picks up a glass and wipes it with his cloth, turning away slightly.

"You always clean glasses that don't need cleaning, or is that your way of pretending I'm not here?"

He glances up, blinking before forcing a tight smile. "Just keeping busy," he mutters. "What can I get you?"

"Lemon gin."

He hesitates. "Pres said no alcohol. Something to do with your sleep meds?"

I groan, rolling my eyes. "Fine. Get me a lemonade."

I turn, scanning the room, and my eyes land on Poison. She's perched on the edge of the pool table, and as if she senses me, we lock eyes.

And then, nothing. No smirk. No snide comment. No slow clap like she's gonna tear me apart. She just picks up her drink and turns her back. I frown. Poison *hates* me. She never misses a chance to throw shade.

I take my lemonade and sit on the couch. It's my usual spot, but this time, it feels different. Like I don't belong. Like the club has moved around me, reshaping itself and forgetting my imprint.

The guys aren't just giving me space. They're afraid of what might happen if they don't.

Bully steps out the office and spots me. He heads over, dropping down beside me. "Why do you look so . . . lost?" he asks. It's been a week since we came back here, and it's not the first time he's found me sitting here alone.

"Bria's gone for a run," I say with a shrug, then I glance around. "Have you told everyone to avoid me?"

He laughs. "Why would I do that?"

"Because they are. Even Poison didn't give me any shit."

He laughs harder. "You're upset because Poison didn't run her mouth off?"

"I just want everything to go back to normal," I mutter, picking at some imaginary lint on my shirt. "Nothing feels normal anymore."

He smiles. "Well, luckily for you, I have something planned to take your mind off all of this." He stands, pulling me with him.

The second we step outside, the air changes. It's quieter, softer. Still with the faint smell of oil and cigarettes, but it's better than inside, where every room feels like it's holding its breath around me.

He leads me around the back of the clubhouse, and I know he's taking me to the tree, the one I like to sit under to read or just think.

I spot the blanket already laid out underneath and smile. I never thought I'd see the day that Bully arranged a picnic. "Okay, where's Liam and what have you done with him?"

"I know you love it out here," he says, kicking off his heavy boots and stepping onto the blanket. "We can watch the sunset and relax, forget everything else for a while."

I sink onto the frayed blanket. "Are you trying to seduce me?"

He grins, sitting next to me. "Is it working?"

I tuck my feet underneath me and release a sigh. For the first time all week, no one is watching me. There's no awkward silences, no eyes darting away.

Just him and me.

"Thank you," I say, barely a whisper. I feel him turn to look at me. "For this. For looking after me since . . . well, yah know." My heart suddenly feels heavy with all the things I want to say but daren't in case I ruin the truce we've found ourselves in.

His hand slides to mine, entwining our fingers together. "It's not easy loving me," he states, "I know that. And you keep loving me, even when I fuck it all up. The least I owe you is to stand by you in your hours of need."

I offer a weak smile, hating how even this moment has turned because of my heavy mood. I stare out to the sunset, its deep orange glow warming my heart. "So, what did you make to eat?"

He eagerly opens the basket and brings out two well-wrapped baguettes. Everything he creates in the kitchen, from a cheese sandwich to a medium rare steak, he's proud of, and I can't help but get swept up in his enthusiasm. "Ham and cheese with salad," he announces, holding one out to me.

I smile gratefully. "My favourite," I lie. He gives me a knowing stare until I laugh. "What?"

"We both know your favourite is peanut butter with a trail of Marmite."

"You swore that was our secret," I say with a mock gasp.

He grins. "I refuse to make such a monstrous sandwich, so enjoy the ham and cheese."

I unwrap it and take a bite. My appetite seems to have picked up, a sign that things are starting to go back to how they were. My nightmares are still plaguing me through the night, and who knows when they'll fade, but the doc gave me some sleeping pills to help.

"Bria and Lords have been together a lot lately," says Bully, side-eyeing me like he's waiting for me to offer up information on my sister.

I shrug. "She's chatty with all the guys. Don't read too much into it."

"No?"

I scoff. "I mean, Bria and Lords? Really? She'd corrupt him and his faith."

Bully laughs, wiping his mouth and throwing his wrapper back in the basket. He leans back on his palms, watching the sunset. I lie back, placing my hands behind my head and staring up at the fading blue sky.

Bully

I glance down at Liv. She's lying back, eyes half-closed, face soft in the evening light. And my heart aches with love. It's been so long since I actually just looked at her. *Really* looked. When we're together like this, I can almost forget that I've lost her.

I clear my throat as my stomach twists tight. I have things I need to say, things she needs to hear. "I was a bastard to you."

Her eyes flick to me, cautious, like she's not sure if I'm being serious or if I'm about to tell her a joke. I twist round so I'm looking down at her. "Not just once. Not just the cheating. Not just the lying or the bullshit excuses. It's all the ways I didn't see you." I take a breath. "You'd walk into the room, and I'd look right past you, Liv. At someone louder. Someone easier. Someone who didn't make me feel things I didn't know what to do with." I scrub my hand over my jaw.

"I thought love was supposed to be messy. Dangerous. Fast. Like a fight you wanted to lose. But you . . . you were patient with me when I didn't deserve it. You gave me so many chances that I pissed away, and you still showed up." I stare out to the sun as it dips behind the trees, then I look back to her. "I don't know how to undo it. I can't go back, but I can stand in front of you now and say I'm sorry." I swallow hard, my voice dipping lower.

"I'm sorry I made you feel small. Invisible. Replaceable. You were never that. Not even for a second. I was just too stupid and too selfish to see what was standing right in front of me." She blinks, her throat bobbing like she's full of emotion. "You deserved better than who I was. And I'm not saying I've figured it all out, but I see you, Liv. *I see you*. And if you'll let me, I want to do better by you. Not just say it . . . *show* it."

Silence settles between us, heavy and charged. But it's out there now. The truth, with no sugar-coated lies. Everything I should have said from the start. Everything I've been wanting to say since I found her sobbing in the shower after Dagger.

She pulls her knees to her chest, resting her chin there and staring out into the distance. "You don't get it," she eventually whispers. She lays her head to the side, watching me closely. "You say you see me now, and maybe you do, but I've spent so long waiting for you that your words feel . . . empty. Like you're saying them because you feel like you should, because you can feel it's different now that I really am ready to walk away." She gives a small, unamused laugh. "Do you even know what it feels like to come second, third even?"

I open my mouth to speak, to tell her I'm serious this time, but she cuts me off. "No, let me finish." I give a nod, remaining silent. "I wanted so badly to be enough for you. And when I wasn't, I told myself I didn't care. That I was tough and could handle it. But secretly, it broke me, bit by bit. *You* broke me. And I still love you." My body stills, dreading her next words. "That's the worst part. I never stopped. I can never seem to stop, even when you were with somebody else. I love you like it's wired into my bones." Her eyes glisten with unshed tears, and she breathes deeply. "But I'm scared, Bully. Terrified that if I let you back in, if I put those pieces in your hands again, you won't hold them together." I exhale a shuddering breath. "I want to forgive you, but I think I'll always be holding back, waiting for you to leave me standing in the dark again."

"I won't," I say simply. "And I don't know how to show that, how to prove it, but I know what it's like to live without you and I hate it. I need you by my side." I carefully brush the hair from her face.

"When I got out, I was desperate to prove to the brothers, to Jameson, that I was worthy to run this club just like my dad, just like Hawk. I threw myself in, trying to prove myself, and I forgot about the most important person in all of it. *You*. Yeah, I can run the club, but without you, I don't want to. You make me the best version of their president. Without you, there's no point in any of it."

"What are you saying?"

I shrug, the words almost choking me. "That if you want me to, I'll walk away." Silence deafens me as I look her in the eye. "I'll step away from the club."

After what feels like forever, she offers a gentle, almost sad smile. "This is your life," she whispers.

"No," I say, shaking my head. "You're my life. Everything I want is with you."

"I don't want you to walk away from this place," she mutters, glancing back at the clubhouse. "It's you," she says simply with a shrug. "And without it, you wouldn't be you anymore. I can handle the club life," she continues, "but if you're going to love me, Bully, it can't be halfway or half in. This time, I need your all."

Hope fills my chest, and I find myself nodding, scared that if I take my eyes off her for a second, she'll change her mind. "There are no more chances after this," she continues. "No more excuses."

"I promise."

Her eyes search my face. "Don't make me look like a fool again."

I lean in, kissing her gently on the cheek, then the lips, soft and slow as I climb over her and push her onto her back. "Never again."

"And we take things slow, until I can trust you fully."

"I won't let you down again, Liv. I'm lucky you're agreeing to give me this chance, and I won't blow it. I am going to treat you like the queen you deserve. No one compares."

EPILOGUE

Olivia

The sun is just starting to dip behind the clubhouse, casting long golden shadows over the carpark like it always does before the night rolls in. That twilight hour, where things soften, where everything feels peaceful.

I settle on the front steps with a notepad balanced on my knees, doodling lazy curves, hearts, and half-formed logos while I brainstorm ways to grow the business. *Our* business. The club's more than just patched jackets and engines now. It's potential. A future.

It's been weeks since Bully and I took that leap again. And now, it's like a distant memory. And he's proving himself every damn day. Even Bria, who once threatened to skin him alive, can't deny the shift. He's not just showing up, he's showing *me* off. Making space. Making amends. Loving out loud.

I glance up, eyes lingering on him, shirtless, sweat-slicked, working on his Harley with that mix of focus and chaos that somehow always undoes me.

He glances over and catches me staring, and he grins that crooked grin that drives me mad. "You staring again, Liv?"

"Obviously," I smirk. "You're the best view out here."

He drops the wrench, wipes his hands on a rag like he's got nowhere else to be but here, and strolls over, cocky, effortless . . . *mine.*

His oil-stained fingers cup my face, thumb brushing my cheek. "Say it again," he murmurs.

"Best. View. Ever."

His kiss is warm, familiar, teasing. Like he's memorising me. And when he pulls back, he's still smiling. "I still don't know how I got so lucky," he murmurs.

"Hard work," I say, tracing his jaw with my fingers, "and multiple orgasms."

He huffs a laugh. "Speaking of orgasms . . ."

His fingers lace through mine, and he tugs me up, wrapping an arm around my waist. We head towards the club, our kingdom, our chaos.

We have scars, some you can see, most you can't. The past still echoes. But love doesn't need to erase it—it just needs to make space around it. For second chances. For rebuilding. For us.

I'm not standing in his shadow anymore. I'm standing *with* him. *Beside* him. As us. His darkness is my light, and my fire is his calm. And this time, I don't have to ask to be seen. Because every day, in every way, he shows me.

The plans I've been scribbling—expanding the garage, opening that community space Bria keeps banging on about, maybe even running self-defence classes for women and girls—they don't feel far off anymore.

They feel *real*.

I am finally, completely, and irreversibly home.

The End

ABOUT THE AUTHOR

Nicola Jane is a romance author from Nottinghamshire, England, with a lifelong love for storytelling. From a young age, she found both comfort and inspiration in books, often escaping into imaginary worlds and crafting short stories of her own during her teenage years.

After a break from writing, Nicola returned to the page, driven by the need to give voice to the characters and stories that had taken root in her imagination. About five years ago, she took a leap of faith and began sharing her work publicly—something she now describes as one of the most rewarding decisions of her life.

Nicola is known for writing emotionally charged, drama-rich romance that doesn't shy away from real-life challenges. Her stories blend intensity with authenticity, capturing the highs and lows of love in all its forms. Her works span subgenres from gritty motorcycle romance to young adult, all available on Amazon and included in Kindle Unlimited.

When she's not writing, Nicola cherishes time with her husband and two teenage children. Their laughter and love provide constant inspiration and grounding beyond the written word.

OTHER SERIES BY THIS AUTHOR

Available Here

The Kings Reapers MC
The Perished Riders MC
The Chaos Demons MC

Printed in Dunstable, United Kingdom